"LET THE WOMEN GO."

"This ain't your business," Jake said.

"I'm making it my business."

"You don't see nobody else buttin' in."

"No," Clint said, "just me." He pointed his gun at Jake. "Let the women go."

Reluctantly and angrily, Jake released the woman he was holding—so violently that she fell to the ground. The other two men let go of the girls they were holding, and instantly two of the other girls helped the one who was half naked and threw a shawl around her. After that they all just looked at Clint.

It seemed as if the whole town was looking at them.

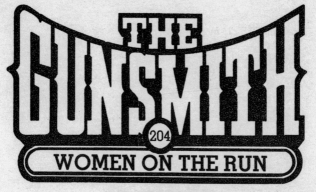

THE GUNSMITH

204

WOMEN ON THE RUN

J. R. ROBERTS

JOVE BOOKS, NEW YORK

WOMEN ON THE RUN

A Jove Book / published by arrangement with
the author

PRINTING HISTORY
Jove edition / January 1999

All rights reserved.
Copyright © 1999 by Robert J. Randisi.
This book may not be reproduced in whole
or in part, by mimeograph or any other means,
without permission. For information address:
The Berkley Publishing Group, a member of Penguin Putnam Inc.,
375 Hudson Street, New York, New York 10014.

The Penguin Putnam Inc. World Wide Web site address is
http://www.penguinputnam.com

ISBN: 0-515-12438-9

A JOVE BOOK®
Jove Books are published by The Berkley Publishing Group,
a member of Penguin Putnam Inc.,
375 Hudson Street, New York, New York 10014.
JOVE and the "J" design are trademarks belonging to
Jove Publications, Inc.

PRINTED IN THE UNITED STATES OF AMERICA

10 9 8 7 6 5 4 3 2 1

PROLOGUE

"The girls want to leave."

Theodore "Ted" Carthage looked up at the woman standing in front of his desk and frowned.

"What?"

"I said the girls want to leave," Gloria Reno said.

"What do you mean, leave?"

"Read my lips, Teddy," Gloria said, leaning across his desk. "They want to leave Carthage County."

She was the only one who ever called him "Teddy," and sometimes the honor made her get carried away with the manner in which she spoke to him. He came out of his chair and backhanded her across the face. The blow sent her staggering back. She banged into a small wooden table, almost knocking it over, and came to rest on a small divan set against the wall. Before she could move he was hovering over her.

"Don't—" she said, holding her hand in front of her face.

"Sometimes you try my patience, Gloria," Ted Carthage said. "Now, very quickly and in a straightforward manner, tell me what the hell you're talking about."

"It's just like I said," she replied, "the girls want to

1

leave Carthage. They want to go. They don't like it here anymore.''

''All of them?'' he asked. ''They all want to leave?''

''Well, no,'' she said. ''Six of them.''

''Which six?''

''Teddy—''

''Which six?!'' he roared. ''Tell me which six whores are the ungrateful whores in my whorehouse!''

''They're not ungrateful,'' she said. ''They just want to move on.''

''In order to move on,'' Carthage said, ''they have to leave me.'' He leaned over her and she cringed, thinking he was going to hit her again. ''And no one leaves me, Gloria. You of all people know that.''

''They're not going to just leave, Tedd—uh, Ted,'' she said, thinking she'd been struck for calling him Teddy at a time when he didn't want to be called that. ''They wanted me to tell you—uh, to ask you if they could leave.''

Carthage straightened up and looked down at her.

''Well,'' he said, ''the answer is no. They can't leave. I need all the whores I have. Ben Swallow is coming in with his men at the end of the week, and you know what they're like.''

Gloria shivered. She did know what Swallow and his men were like. They were the cruelest of all the men who came to Carthage House. They always left several girls so bruised and battered that they couldn't work for a week afterward—something that made Carthage very angry at them. Good God, she thought, why does he think they want to leave before Swallow and his men get here?

What she hadn't told him—what she dared not tell him—was that she wanted to leave, too. She was Carthage's madam, at thirty-three not that far removed from the beds herself. And, in fact, she was still pressed into action when groups like Swallow and his men came to town. Just the thought of Big Ben Swallow's massive hands on her made her shiver again.

"Are you cold?" Carthage asked.

"No, Ted," she said, straightening in her chair. His demeanor had changed, and she now knew he wasn't going to strike her again.

"You're shivering," he said. "Are you sick? You're not going to make my girls sick, are you?"

"No, Ted," she said, "I'm not sick."

"Well, you go and tell those girls they can't leave," Carthage said, "not just yet, anyway."

Suddenly, hope flared inside of her.

"You mean you might let them leave eventually?" she asked.

"We'll talk about it after Ben and his crew leave," Carthage said. "If Ben was to get here and the girls were gone, he'd kill me and burn the town to the ground. You wouldn't want that, would you, Gloria? Would your girls want that?"

"No, Ted," Gloria said, "they wouldn't."

"There you go, then," Carthage said. He straightened his vest and walked around behind his desk. He was a tall, handsome man in his forties, his thick black hair flecked with gray these days. He had found Gloria Reno in a whorehouse in New Orleans and convinced her to come and work for him in Carthage City, Missouri. That was two years ago, when she was thirty-one and tired of working the beds herself. She'd been at it for eight years and felt it was starting to tell on her looks. Even she admitted that she was no longer as beautiful as she had been when she was twenty, but she was still a handsome woman, with a woman's lush curves and eyes that were still clear and blue and not smudged with shadow. She knew many women who grew dark shadows beneath their eyes that no amount of makeup could cover, and she had wanted to get out of the business before that happened. She'd thought Carthage was her way out, but found herself—in some ways—in a worse hell than she had ever been.

"You go and tell the girls, Gloria," he said. "And I'm sorry I hit you. You made me mad."

"Sure, Ted," she said, standing and moving toward the door. Lately, he'd get mad at the drop of a hat. "That's okay. I'll—I'll tell the girls, and I'll see you later."

Ted Carthage was looking down at his desk, Gloria and her girls already forgotten, as she slipped out of the room.

The girls were waiting anxiously for Gloria to return.

"What if he says no?" Miriam Walker asked. At nineteen, she was the youngest of the six prostitutes who wanted to leave Carthage.

"What do you think he's gonna say?" Ally Dixie asked. "You think a man who named a county after himself, and every town in it, is just gonna let us go?"

There were five towns in Carthage County: Carthage Crossing, Carthage Mill, Carthage Circle, Carthageville, and Carthage City. At that moment the girls were in Carthage City, the largest of the five. This was where Ted Carthage chose to set up his whorehouse and his biggest saloon.

"So then what do we do?" Miriam asked.

"Girl," Jennalee Miller said, "we leavin' no matter what the man say." Jennalee was the only black whore in the place. Ted Carthage was especially going to miss her. He himself had been surprised at how popular the black whore was with white men.

"That's right," Rachel Dolan said. "No way I'm staying here any longer."

"Wait," Kathy Cutter said. She was at the window, looking out. Now she turned and said excitedly, "Gloria's comin' back."

The girls waited while Gloria entered the house, came up the stairs, and made her way to the room they were all in, which was Kathy's.

The minute Gloria entered Miriam asked anxiously, "What'd he say?"

The other four girls, older than Miriam—ranging in ages

from twenty-two to twenty-nine—knew from looking at Gloria what the answer was.

"He said no," she said finally. "We can't leave."

"Did you tell him you wanted to leave, too?" Rachel asked.

"You didn't tell him which of us wanted to leave, did you?" Jennalee asked.

"No, I didn't," she said. "He asked, but I was able to get out without telling him."

"How did you manage that?" Ally asked.

"I told him we—you—weren't planning to leave, you were just asking."

"And he said no," Kathy said.

"He said you couldn't leave because . . ."

"Why?" Miriam asked.

"Because Ben Swallow and his men were coming to town at the end of the week."

"That's it," Jennalee said, rising from the bed and stamping her foot. "I ain't lettin' one of them crazy white men put his hands on me again. I'm leavin' . . . tonight!" She turned to face the other girls. "Who's comin' with me?"

None of them answered.

"Rachel?"

No answer.

"Kathy?"

Still no answer.

"Miriam? Come on, baby, you can't stay here. Those men always hurt you." *'Cause you ask for it,* she thought to herself, *with your baby face and meek attitude, you ask for it.*

"Jennalee," Gloria said. "You can't."

"What?"

"You can't leave."

"You gonna stop me?"

"I mean," Gloria said, "you can't leave tomorrow. It's only Monday. We need time to prepare. I'll go with you, but let's take the next couple of days to prepare, and we'll leave Thursday.''

"Prepare for what?"

"We'll need supplies," Gloria said.

"And food," Rachel chimed in.

"And a wagon," Kathy said.

"And if I wait," Jennalee asked, "you'll all go?"

They all answered yes in turn, some spoken, some just by nodding.

Jennalee turned and faced Gloria.

"All right," she said, "I'll wait."

"Good," Gloria said, "then here's what we'll do. . . ."

ONE

Six weeks later ...

When Clint rode into Cotswold, Wyoming, it was to give himself a rest as much as his big gelding, Duke. It was a rare time when both of them were tuckered out at the same time, but that was the case just now.

That was yesterday, when they arrived. Today Duke was in the livery and Clint was in the saloon, both getting the rest they deserved. Clint had had a good night's sleep on a real bed—or as real as the hotel had. The mattress was kind of thin, but it was better than the ground he'd been sleeping on, and the pillow wasn't much, but it was better than using his saddle as one.

Now he was letting his lunch settle, enjoying an early afternoon beer in the all but empty saloon. He and two other men were the only ones drinking, and the other men were sitting at a table together playing poker head-to-head.

"Hey, mister?" one of them called over.

Clint ignored him. He'd been hoping to get through this day without having to speak to anyone but a waiter, room clerk, or bartender, and then head out early the next morning. He thought if he ignored these fellas they'd take the hint.

"Hey!" one of them called. "I'm talkin' ta you."

"Leave 'im be, Jake," the other man said. "Maybe he don't hear you."

"He hears jest fine," the man called Jake said. "Hey, friend, me and my pard here would like to play poker, but not this heads up crap. You wanna sit in?"

Clint finally turned his head and looked at the man.

"No, thanks."

He turned away.

"Son of a—" Jake said. "First he ignores me, now he's too good to play poker with us."

"He don't wanna play, Jake," the other man said. "So what?"

"Hey, you!" Jake said, ignoring his friend. "You too good to play poker with us?"

Clint answered, this time without looking at the man.

"Your friend is right."

"Huh?"

"I don't want to play poker with you," Clint said. "So what?"

"Are you talkin' ta me?" Jake demanded. Clint heard the man's chair scrape the floor as he got up. "Goddamn it, if you're talkin' ta me you should be lookin' at me, friend."

"Jake—" his friend called.

Clint turned his head in time to see the man coming at him—but before he could react another man burst into the saloon.

"Jake, Al!" he said. "I found 'em. They're here."

Jake froze, and Al got up.

"Come on, Jake," Al said. He put his hand on Jake's arm. Jake was still glaring at Clint. "Jake! Sam's found 'em. Come on!"

"Jake!" the third man, Sam, called.

Jake spoke to Clint.

"This ain't over, mister."

Clint looked at him.

"As far as I'm concerned, it never started," he said. "Let's keep it that way, friend."

"Oh, it started all right, *friend,* and I'll be back to finish it, so you just wait there for me."

Clint just raised his half finished glass of beer.

"When this is done, I'm gone."

"Come on, Jake!" Al said, moving to the door.

"I'll find you, friend," Jake said, following his partner. "Don't you worry, I'll find you, just as soon as my business here is finished."

Clint couldn't help but wonder what kind of business allowed a man to waste time in a saloon playing two-handed poker and picking foolish fights that were going to get him killed.

TWO

Clint finished his beer at a leisurely pace—but not too leisurely. Finishing it too fast, or too slow, would both send the wrong message. He wasn't looking for a fight, but he couldn't afford to run from one, either.

About fifteen minutes after the two men had left, he could hear the sounds of a commotion outside on the street. The bartender came around from behind the bar and went to the door to see what was happening.

"What's going on?" Clint asked.

"Looks like those two who just left and their friend are dragging some women out into the street."

"What?"

Clint got up to take a look for himself. He stepped outside and saw what the bartender was talking about. Each of the men had a woman by the arm and was pulling them. Two of the women were dragging their feet, the other was simply being dragged. Three other women were following, screaming at the men to stop. None of the women were dressed to be on the street.

"Nobody's stopping them," Clint said.

"What for?" the bartender asked. "They're whores."

Clint looked at him.

"And that makes a difference?"

11

"Don't it?" the man asked.

Clint cursed under his breath. If nobody was going to do anything to help, it was going to be up to him.

He stepped down off the boardwalk and started walking toward the action, which had drawn a crowd. The towns-women were looking on with disapproval, while the men were whooping and hollering because the six women weren't dressed. In fact, the girl who was being dragged was half naked as her top had been torn away and her breasts were bobbing free, covered with dirt from the street. She looked to be no more than twenty, if that.

Clint reached them and could hear the other women shouting.

"Leave them alone," one said.

"You have no right!"

"We got every right," one of the men said. It was Jake, the man who wanted to pick a fight with Clint. "You whores belong to Carthage."

"We belong to nobody," another woman yelled.

Suddenly, a black woman in a flimsy green gown charged Jake and tried to rake his eyes with her nails. He swung a backhand at her, knocking her to the ground.

"Nigger whore!" he shouted.

"Hold it!" Clint yelled, but nobody could hear him. As the black woman hit the ground and the others closed around her the crowd got louder. Clint looked around, but there wasn't a badge toter anywhere.

He drew his gun and fired into the air, and it got real quiet.

THREE

"You!" Jake said, when he recognized Clint from the saloon.

"Me," Clint said. "Let the women go."

"This ain't your business," Jake said.

"I'm making it my business."

"You don't see nobody else buttin' in."

"No," Clint said, "just me." He pointed his gun at Jake. "Let the women go."

Reluctantly and angrily, Jake released the woman he was holding—so violently that she fell to the ground. The other two men let go of the girls they were holding, and instantly two of the other girls helped up the one who was half naked and threw a shawl around her. After that they all just looked at Clint.

It seemed as if the whole town was looking at him.

"Isn't there a lawman in this town?" he called out.

"I'm the law."

A man wearing a badge stepped into the street. He had a bored look on his face, and his gun was still holstered. He had a beer belly that hung over his belt, and his skin was pasty white. He looked drunk. He must have been in another saloon or else drinking in his office when the commotion started.

13

"Aren't you going to do anything about this?" Clint asked.

"About what?"

"These men are manhandling these women."

"They're whores," the lawman said. "They get paid to be manhandled."

"Not dragged through the street," Clint said.

"Ain't my business."

"Sheriff," Jake said, "we got a right to defend ourselves, don't we?"

"You got a right," the lawman said, "but it ain't a fair fight 'cause he's got his gun drawn already."

"It's three against one," one of the women, a blonde who looked older than the rest, called out.

"Still," the sheriff said, "it ain't fair he's got his gun out." He looked at Clint. "Mister, you holster that gun. If you don't and you shoot one of these gents, I'm gonna have to take you in."

"And if they shoot me after I holster my weapon?"

"Hey," the sheriff said, "you stuck your nose in their business. Who asked you to do that?"

"Sheriff, you can't—" the blond woman said.

"Shut up, whore!" Jake shouted, turning to face Clint. The other men—Sam and Al—did the same, tight smiles on their faces. "He's the law, so you just shut up."

"Holster it, mister," the sheriff said.

If he didn't, Clint knew he'd be in violation of the law. If he did, the three men were going to draw on him.

"Whatever you say, Sheriff," he said, and holstered the gun.

"Okay, then," the sheriff said.

"This fair, Sheriff?" Jake called out.

"Fair as I can see it," the sheriff said, looking around and drawing approval from the people who were watching.

"Sheriff," Clint said, "let these women get off the street and out of the line of fire."

"Why not?" the sheriff said. "Go ahead, *ladies,*" he

said with exaggerated politeness, "get off the street."

The women began to move off the street, some helping others, and the blond one looked at Clint.

"I sure appreciate your help, mister," she said, "but I'm sorry you got into this."

"That's okay, miss," Clint said. "Just get off the street."

She nodded and did so.

"You, too, Sheriff," Clint said, "unless you're siding with them."

"Not siding with anybody," the sheriff said, lifting his hands high and backing up until he could step up onto the boardwalk.

Now the town was watching, waiting for the action to take place. Some of them were holding their breath, others were making bets, but they were all watching.

"Any time, mister," Jake said. "I told you I'd get back to you."

"Shut up and do it," Clint said.

The three men went for their guns together. Clint's practiced eye picked out the fastest of the three—Al—and he shot him first. There was little to pick between the other two, and little time to do it, anyway, so he simply shot Sam, and then Jake.

They all fell to the ground, their guns still in their holsters, except for Al, whose gun was on the ground.

It was very quiet, and then all of the women—the whores—started to whoop and holler.

Clint holstered his gun and walked over to where the sheriff was standing. The crowd around the man dispersed, as he shrank back from the look on Clint's face.

"You got a problem with what just happened, *Sheriff*?" he demanded.

"N-no, s-sir," the sheriff said. "Fair's fair."

"Burying these men is your responsibility, then," Clint said, "and I'd better see their graves before I leave town tomorrow morning."

With that Clint turned and drew his gun from his holster again, but only long enough to eject the empties and reload. Then he walked across the street to where the six women were standing.

"Are you all right?" he asked.

"We're fine," the blond woman said. "That was ... amazing."

"Are you all right, miss?" he asked the girl who had been dragged.

"Yes," she said timidly.

"And you?" he asked the black girl.

"Take more than some white man's backhand to hurt me," she said.

"Well, that's good," he said.

"Did I hear you say you were leaving tomorrow?" the blonde asked.

"That's right."

"We are, too," she said. "Would you ride with us while we leave?"

"If you're ready early," he said. "I don't see why not."

"We'll be ready," she said. "We'll all be traveling in one wagon."

"Meet me at the livery about eight, then," Clint said. "If you're not there I'll be on my way."

"We'll be there, mister," the blonde said. "My name is Gloria. I'll introduce you to the rest of the girls tomorrow."

"That's fine," he said. "My name's Clint."

The girl with the shawl covering her suddenly moved to him, stood on tiptoe and kissed his cheek.

"Thank you," she said.

"You're welcome."

"Come on, girls," Gloria said, "let's get packed. We're leaving in the morning."

As the other girls turned and started back into the building they had been dragged out of, Gloria turned to Clint again.

"They were right, you know."

"Who was?"

"Those men," she said. "We are whores. Does that make a difference?"

"It doesn't to me, if it doesn't to you," Clint said.

She smiled and said, "See you in the morning."

FOUR

As promised the women were at the livery when Clint arrived. In fact, they were all in the wagon, smiling at him when he got there. He greeted them all, went in to saddle Duke, and then rode him out. The women oohed and aahed over the big black gelding, and then they started their ride out of town. Most of the town was watching the day before when they were being dragged into the street. Today no one watched as they left.

"I hope you're properly outfitted for your trip," he said, "wherever it is you're going."

"We didn't have much money," Gloria said. She was driving the wagon and the timid-looking girl—who had been introduced as Miriam—was riding next to her. "We have a few supplies, though."

"How about where you're going?" he asked.

"We don't know."

"You didn't plan?"

"Plan?" Gloria asked. "Yesterday morning we didn't know we'd be leaving today. If those men hadn't—" She started but stopped abruptly, as if she'd been just about to tell him something she didn't want to tell him.

"But they're dead," he said.

19

"If they found us," Miriam said, "others will," before Gloria silenced her with a look.

"Where am I taking you, then?" Clint asked.

Gloria reined in the team and turned to look at him. Some of the women peeked out behind her from the covered Conestoga, and others looked out the back to see why they had stopped.

"You should probably know this before we go any further," she said. "There are other men looking for us. A lot of them."

"And they work for Carthage?"

She looked startled that he would know that name.

"How did you—"

"I heard one of the men say it yesterday, that you all belonged to Carthage."

"We all worked for him," Gloria said, "in Missouri. When we decided to leave he didn't want us to. We sneaked away."

"With the wagon?"

She nodded.

"It wasn't easy. We only had two days, but we put together whatever supplies and money we could, stole this wagon, and left."

Clint rubbed his jaw.

"Well, I doubt that he's after you for stealing the wagon."

"No," Gloria said, "but he'll use that as an excuse. He really just wants us all back working for him, and we're tired of it."

"But in town, weren't you still—"

"We're tired of working for *him*," she said, "not tired of working."

"I see."

"So you also see that you're in danger if you stay with us. I saw you shoot down three men yesterday and it was amazing, but next time there might be more than three. We don't know where we're going, but as far as where you're taking us, you can leave us right now.''

"No," Clint said with a sigh, "I can't."

"Why not?"

"Because you're six women alone, with men after you," Clint said. "How could I live with myself if I left you alone?"

"You mean you'll stay with us?" Miriam asked happily.

"Until I see you to someplace safe," he said.

"And where is that?" Gloria asked. "Where are we gonna be safe from Theodore Carthage?"

"I don't know," Clint said. "I guess that's just something we're going to have to figure out together, isn't it?"

FIVE

They traveled most of the day, the only request by Gloria and the other girls being that they keep going west. To head east would bring them too close to Missouri.

"Maybe he wouldn't expect that," Clint suggested.

"He'd hear about us," she said. "It's not easy for six women traveling together."

"Maybe you should think about that."

"About what?" she asked.

Miriam was driving the wagon at this point, with Gloria taking a rest. Duke was so big that riding next to the wagon Clint was almost sitting right beside Gloria. They were able to speak in normal tones.

"Splitting up."

They both heard Miriam's sharp intake of breath, and Gloria put her hand on the younger girl's arm momentarily to soothe her.

"We have to stay together," Gloria said.

"But if that's part of the problem—"

"You see," Gloria said, "separated, we're not strong enough. Take Miriam. If we split up she's the first one who would end up back in Carthage County. In fact, she'd probably *go* back because she wouldn't know where else to go."

"And the others?" Clint asked. "Some of them seem strong enough."

"Two or three might be," Gloria said, "but what about the others? See, they've been my girls for a long time. I have to take care of them."

Clint had known from the start that Gloria was the stronger of the six. He thought, also, that the black girl—Jennalee—was, too. She was the only one who had actually attacked Jake when he was pulling on one of the girls—Rachel, as it turned out. He didn't know about the others yet.

"I see," he said, and dropped the subject of splitting up.

They stopped for lunch, but it was a cold camp. They all agreed they could wait until supper for hot food and coffee. Before long, they were moving again.

Gloria and Miriam had moved into the back and now Jennalee was driving the rig, with Rachel next to her. Slowly, as the day wore on, he was getting the names right.

"Can I ask you somethin'?" Jennalee asked.

"Sure."

"Did you know you was gonna be able to kill those men? I mean, you knew you could outdraw *three* men?"

"I had a pretty good idea."

"It was the damnedest thing I ever did see, I gotta tell you," she said, shaking her head.

He didn't say anything. In fact, he was hoping she'd drop the whole thing.

But she didn't.

"You done that before?"

"Once or twice."

"Do I know you?"

"I'm sorry?"

"Should I know who you are?" she asked. "What's your full name?"

"Adams," he said, "Clint Adams." It was the first time any of them had asked him.

"Well, goddamn," she said. "The Gunsmith, right?"

"That's right."

"Holy shit," she said, "we got the goddamn Gunsmith as a bodyguard."

Clint didn't reply.

"There's still somethin' I don't know, though," she said.

"What's that?"

"Why?"

"Why what?"

"Why you did it," she said. "Why you're doin' this, helpin' us."

"I did it in town because you needed it," Clint said, "and nobody else was offering. I'm doing it now because you still need it."

"And you don't expect nothin' in return?"

"No."

"Nothin'?"

"No."

"You mean you got a wagon full of whores here and you don't—"

"No," he said, cutting her off, "I don't. I'm going to scout up ahead some."

"Oh, you don't got to do that," she said. "I'll shut up for a while."

"Promise?" he asked her.

She flashed her white teeth at him in a dazzling smile and said, "I promise."

SIX

When they camped for the night Clint saw that the women had their routine down pat. Two of them—Miriam and Kathy, he thought—took care of the fire and the food. Jennalee and Rachel took care of the wagon and the horses. Gloria and Ally put out everyone's blankets and bedrolls for the night. Maybe, he thought, he'd finally gotten everyone's names right.

Clint took care of Duke himself, but he benefited from the girls' routine when Miriam handed him a plate of bacon and beans.

"Thank you," he said.

"You're welcome." She looked away shyly, but during the course of the day Clint had caught her staring at him more than once. It was not the first time a whore had ever gotten a crush on him. He'd saved her from the bad men, though, and at her age that was enough to convince her that she was in love. It would pass.

"It'll pass," Gloria said, sitting next to him with her own plate.

"What?"

"Miriam's crush on you," Gloria said. "It'll pass, in time."

"Are you a mind reader?"

"No," she said, "but I read faces. She has a crush on you, and you're wondering how to handle it."

"And the answer is?"

"You don't have to," she said. "It will go away all by itself. Surely you've had experience with young crushes before."

"Once or twice."

"What did you do then?"

He smiled.

"I talked to the girls' fathers."

Gloria laughed.

"Well, no fathers around here," she said, shaking her head. "I guess I'm the closest thing to it, the mother figure."

"You're not old enough to be mother to any of these women," he said.

"Thank God for that," she said. "Miriam's very young, though, only nineteen."

"How long has she been . . ."

"A whore?"

He nodded.

"About a year, I guess," Gloria said. "The other girls and I have been together a little longer. Carthage brought her in a year ago, and we all sort of adopted her."

"Tell me about Carthage . . . if you will?"

"The man? The town? The county? It doesn't matter really, they're all the same. He's got a lot of money, came by it the easy way by inheriting it from his father. Soon as he had it all to himself he began buying up land. Soon enough he had bought the whole county and changed the name. Then he started taking over towns or building 'em, and he named those after himself. Then he started the whorehouse and the saloons, hired himself some sheriffs for his towns, appointed a mayor for each town, but he runs everything."

"Sounds like he's carved out a nice little niche for himself."

Miriam came over with two cups of coffee, handed them each one and gave Gloria an odd look before she smiled at Clint and turned to walk away.

"Uh-oh," Gloria said.

"What?"

"I know that look," Gloria said, putting her coffee on the ground by her feet. "She thinks I'm trying to steal you."

"That's silly—"

"I'll talk to her later," she said. "Don't worry."

"So what made you all want to leave Carthage?" Clint asked.

"Well, first of all we didn't all leave. Some of the girls chose to stay behind."

"Why?"

"They either didn't want to be hunted," Gloria said, "or they decided that they'd make a lot more money once the six of us were gone."

"So why did the six of you leave?"

"We got tired of being brutalized," Gloria said. "It wasn't like that in the beginning, but more and more the men who came to see us decided that hitting us was just as much fun as . . . as fucking us. Then Ted—that's Carthage—started to hit me, and I decided I was leaving. Since I was in charge—the madam, for want of a better word—I had to tell these girls. They're the ones I'm closest to."

"And they all decided to go with you?"

"More or less," Gloria said. "One or two of them needed to be talked into it, but that's about the way it was."

"And when was that?"

"About six weeks ago."

"And he's been hunting you?"

"Not him personally, but he's using Ben Swallow and his men."

"Ben Swallow," Clint said. "I know that name. He and his men are vigilantes."

"They call themselves bounty hunters."

"And it's Swallow and his men who are after you?"

"That's what we heard."

"So I killed three of Ben Swallow's men?"

"I'm not sure if they worked for Swallow or Carthage," Gloria said. "Either way, if word gets back to either of them, they're not gonna like it."

"I guess not."

"Still want to see us to someplace safe?" she asked.

"I don't feel as if I have much choice in the matter," he said. "I can't just leave you all alone. Do you even have a gun with you?"

"No."

"How'd you manage to last six weeks?"

"Lucky, I guess."

"Well," he said, "before I see you to someplace safe, we're going to have to decide on where that is. We can't just wander aimlessly. Maybe we should talk to the other girls and see where they want to go."

"We could do that," she said, "but getting the six of us to agree to anything is kind of hard."

"If you're going to survive," he said, "you're either going to have to be able to agree, or you're going to have to choose someone to make all the decisions for the group. And if you do that, then everybody has to abide by that decision."

They each put down their empty plates and picked up their coffee.

"I would think that would be you," he said.

"Well," she said, "you might get an argument from one or two girls on that."

"Oh?"

"Yeah," she said, "there are those who don't think I've done such a great job taking us this far."

"Well," Clint said, "when everybody's finished eating, why don't we find out what they want to do."

"Suits me," she said. "I'll let everyone know."

She got up to go and talk to the other girls, and Clint watched all of them, thinking how lucky a man he'd be to be with six whores if all they had to do was enjoy one another.

SEVEN

When everyone had finished eating they gathered around the fire, as if someone were going to tell them ghost stories.

"We have to come to a decision," Gloria said to them.

"About what?" Jennalee asked.

Clint instinctively knew that most of the resistance would come from the beautiful but seemingly bitter black girl.

"About where we're going," Gloria said. "About what we're going to do. About whether or not we're going to stay together."

"I thought we were," Miriam said, and then shrank back when everyone looked at her. "I mean, I thought we decided that."

"I think what Gloria means," Rachel said, "is that we need a plan."

"Is that what Gloria says?" Jennalee asked. "Or what this white man says?"

"What does it matter that he's white?" Miriam asked.

"Shut up, Miriam!" Jennalee said.

"Don't tell her to shut up," Rachel said.

"So what if it's Clint's idea," Kathy spoke up. "We need to decide something. We can't go on the way we have been, stopping someplace and then up and running at a moment's notice."

"So what should we do?" Ally asked.

"Jennalee's right," Gloria said. "It was Clint who said we need a definite plan. He also said we'd be smart to split up. I already told him that, to some of us, that's out of the question."

"Let Clint talk," Rachel said.

"Yes," Ally said, "let's hear what he has to say from his own mouth."

"Why do you think we should split up?" Kathy asked.

Gloria turned, looked at Clint, and then sat down to let him take center stage. He did so without moving from his spot.

"First of all," he said, "six women traveling alone attracts a lot of attention. Second, without someplace specific in mind you attract attention by just wandering. You all need to decide what you want to do, or you need to pick someone to make those decisions for you."

"Like Gloria?" Jennalee demanded.

"Whoever you choose," Clint said. "I only met you yesterday, so I can't say who that someone should be. You have to first decide if you want that, and then decide who it should be."

"I think it should be me," Jennalee said.

"I think it should be Gloria," Miriam said, and then shrank back from Jennalee's glare.

"Why should it be one person?" Rachel asked. "We all have minds of our own."

"Rachel's right," Gloria said. "Why don't we all decide where we want to go. We can sleep on it and discuss it again tomorrow." She looked at Clint. "One more day's not going to hurt."

"No," Clint said, "I suppose not."

"Let's get some sleep," Gloria said. "We'll need two girls to alternate watches with Clint so he can get some sleep. I'll take one watch."

"I'll take the other," Jennalee said quickly. Obviously,

she didn't want Gloria to look better than her in front of the other girls.

Miriam and Rachel pitched their bedrolls under the wagon. Ally and Kathy put theirs on the other side of the fire from Clint's. Gloria's and Jennalee's were on the same side as Clint's. That way they wouldn't have to walk across camp to wake each other for their watch.

Clint said, "I'll take the first watch. I'll wake Gloria, and then she can wake you, Jennalee."

"Fine," the black girl said, and wrapped herself in her blanket.

"Don't know what we accomplished tonight," Gloria said to Clint.

"And I guess we won't know until tomorrow," he said. "Get some sleep. I'll wake you in three hours."

"Good night," she said, and turned over to get comfortable.

Idly, Clint wondered why none of the women were sleeping in the wagon.

EIGHT

When Jennalee woke Clint the next morning it was roughly, with her foot.

"Time to get up," she called.

"I'm up," he said, sitting and looking around him. Gloria was also awake, but the other four women were still asleep.

"Wouldn't it make sense for someone to sleep in the wagon?" he asked.

"We went through that," Gloria said.

"We decided that no one should," Jennalee said, "because we couldn't decide *who* should."

Clint frowned. These women had more problems than they thought.

Clint got up and accepted the cup of coffee Gloria handed him.

"What about the others?" he asked.

"We'll wake them in a minute," Gloria said. "Jennalee and I were talking before we woke you up."

"About what?"

"What we were talking about last night," the black girl said.

Both women were facing him, and he had the opportunity to compare them. Gloria was in her early thirties, and

Jennalee looked like she was almost thirty. Both were tall,
both striking: Gloria golden and pale, Jennalee dark all
over. Gloria was more full-bodied, though, while Jennalee
looked sleek and slender, although she did have large
breasts and a rounded butt. Jennalee's hair was very short
while Gloria's stopped just before it touched her shoulders.
Both looked not only beautiful but intelligent.

"What decision did you come to?" he asked.

The two women exchanged a look and in it Clint saw
more cooperation than he had seen the night before.

"We talked about where we'd like to go," Gloria said.
"Jennalee favors New Orleans."

"And you?"

"New York."

"So what did you decide?"

"San Francisco," Jennalee said.

"Is that some sort of compromise?"

"It is," Gloria said.

"San Francisco will have everything New York or New
Orleans would have . . . won't it?" Jennalee asked.

"Oh, I'm sure it will," Clint said. "But it's one thing
to ride into a town like Cotswold and set up shop. What
are you going to do in San Francisco?"

"Once we get there," Jennalee said, "everyone can do
whatever they want. Those that want to stick together can.
Those that want to go their own way can."

"The important thing is to get there safely," Gloria said.

"That's where you come in," Jennalee said.

"Me?"

"You said you wanted to see us safely somewhere,"
Gloria said.

"I know," he said, "but I was thinking of something a
little smaller and a little closer."

"We can make San Francisco on our own," Jennalee
said. "All we need is for you to point us there."

Clint remained silent and sipped his coffee. He loved San

Francisco; it was one of his favorite places. Also, he knew
people there, people who could help these women get settled. And he hadn't been going anywhere in particular when
he entered Cotswold and met the six women. In addition,
he wouldn't have to ride Duke all the way. He could take
a turn driving the wagon while Duke tagged along behind.
Not having Clint's weight on him would be a rest.

"What are you thinking?" Gloria asked.

"You're the mind reader," Clint said to her. "You tell
me."

"You're thinking San Francisco is always an interesting
place to be."

"Have you been there?" he asked.

"No," she said, "but I'd be willing to bet you have."

"And you'd be right."

"So you'll do it?" Jennalee asked.

"On one condition," he said.

"I knew it," the black girl said.

"What condition?" Gloria asked.

Clint looked at Jennalee.

"You and I have to become friends."

She put her hands on her hips.

"In the back of the wagon, I suppose?"

"No," he said, "I said friends. Just stop looking at me
like I'm the enemy."

She looked down at the ground.

"I'm sorry," she said. "Sometimes it's . . . hard."

"I understand that," he said. "All I'm asking is that you
try."

"Can you do that, Jennalee?" Gloria asked.

She looked up at both of them and said, "Okay, I can
do that."

"Good," Clint said. He dumped the remnants of his coffee into the fire. "You'd better wake the others and see if
they'll go along with it, as well."

"And if they do?" Gloria asked.

"We'll have to outfit for a trip to San Francisco," he said. "We'll need enough so that we don't have to make any more stops along the way. It'll be safer that way."

"Okay," Gloria said. "Let's wake 'em up, Jenny!"

NINE

Ted Carthage was having a drink in his saloon in Carthage City when Ben Swallow walked in. The big man spotted him and stomped over. It was the way Ben Swallow walked, always stomping in or out of a room.

"We gotta talk," he said, his tone more guttural than usual.

"Sit down," Carthage said. "I'll get you a beer."

He waved at the bartender, who appeared with one and put it in front of Swallow. Carthage poured himself another shot of whiskey.

"What's wrong?"

"Three of my men are dead."

"How did that happen?"

"They were gunned."

"Where?"

"Some pisshole called Cotswold."

"Where is that?"

"Wyoming."

"What's that got to do with anything?"

"Four of my men were in that town," Swallow said. His jaw was square and covered with gray stubble. His shoulders looked as if they were going to burst the seams of his jacket.

"And three were killed?"

"That's right."

"What did the fourth one do?"

"He watched and reported back by telegraph. My men found your women and were bringin' them back when a man stopped them."

Carthage put his glass down.

"One man?"

"That's right."

"Killed three of yours?"

"In a fair fight," Swallow said. "He outdrew them clean and killed 'em. Al Henry was a good hand with a gun, too."

"And what about the women?"

"They left town the next day with the man."

Carthage laughed.

"So they have a champion now," he said. "One man who can outdraw three."

"There's only two men who could have done that," Swallow said, "and one of them is dead."

"Who's the other one?"

"Clint Adams."

Carthage frowned.

"Wait, I know—oh, the one they call the Gunsmith?"

"That's right."

"Ho," Carthage said, "this is getting really interesting."

"I'm glad you think so," Swallow said. "I lost three men."

"And where's the fourth right now? Is he following them?"

"Hell no, he ain't following them," Swallow said. "He's too damn scared to follow them, and I don't blame 'im."

"What are you telling me, Ben?" Carthage asked. "You going to call your men off?"

"I didn't sign on to have my men killed just to bring back your whores."

"You and your men use my whores, Ben," Carthage said, "and I'm paying you good money to find them and bring them back. I thought you and your men could track anybody."

"We can."

"Then track them."

"It's gonna cost more," Swallow said, "if you want us to go up against the Gunsmith."

Carthage brought his fist down on the table.

"I don't care what it costs!" he said. "I want my whores."

"I'm going myself," Swallow said. "All we got to do is agree on a price."

"You bring them back, Ben," Carthage said. "I guarantee you a fair price."

Swallow stared at Carthage.

"I've never cheated you to this point."

"No," Swallow said, "no, you ain't, and you won't, if you know what's good for you."

"Just bring them back, Ben," Carthage said. "Bring them back here."

"They'll be back," Swallow said, standing, "but it sure beats me why you can't just hire six more whores."

"Not for you to worry about, Ben," Carthage said. "Not for you to worry about."

After Ben Swallow had gone Carthage poured himself another drink from the bottle. The last thing he was going to do was tell someone like Ben Swallow the real reason he wanted those whores back. What they took from him could not be replaced by hiring six more whores.

He especially wanted to get his hands on Gloria Reno. She was behind the whole thing, he knew. All the time she was telling him that six of his whores wanted to leave him, she was one of the six. Those others, they wouldn't have budged without Gloria. She was the ringleader, and she was the one who took what was his.

And Gunsmith or no Gunsmith, he was going to get it back.

TEN

When the other women awoke they were greeted with the news that Gloria and Jennalee had formed a kind of alliance and had come to a decision.

"So you're deciding for us?" Rachel asked.

"Yes," Gloria said.

"Together?" Kathy asked, looking surprised.

"Yes," Jennalee said.

They looked at Clint, who held up his hands.

"Don't look at me," he said. "They told me the same thing when I woke up."

"I'll go wherever you say, Gloria," Miriam said.

"Ally?" Gloria asked.

Ally looked at Jennalee.

"You agree with this?"

"I do," she said. "Somebody has to decide, and we decided to do it together."

"Okay, then," Ally said. "I've got no better ideas. I'll go along."

Jennalee looked at Kathy.

"I'm in," she said.

"Rachel?" Gloria asked.

"Hell," she said, "I'm not going off by myself out here. I'll go along."

"Okay, good," Gloria said. "Then we'd better get started."

"Where are we going?" Ally asked.

"San Francisco," Jennalee said.

"San Francisco?" Miriam said. "How are we going to get there?"

"Clint's going to take us," Gloria said.

"Really?" Miriam asked, delighted.

"Really," Clint said.

"All the way?"

"All the way," Clint said, "but first we need supplies."

"And where do we get those?" Rachel asked.

"The next town."

"And what do we use for money?" Kathy asked.

"I assumed you ladies had some money put away," Clint said, looking at Gloria and Jennalee.

"We've got some," Gloria said.

"Enough for this," Jennalee said.

"Then let's get loaded up," Clint said. "We've got a long trip ahead of us."

The girls scattered, each to do their duty in breaking camp. Miriam, however, came over to Clint, looked at him adoringly, touched his arm and said, "Thank you."

As she walked away Gloria came over and said, "It will pass."

"So you keep saying."

ELEVEN

The next town they came to was called Athens, Wyoming. They stopped just outside of town, at the population sign, to discuss their options.

"From the looks of their population it's a fairly good-sized town," Clint said. "It should have everything we need."

"Then why don't we go in?" Gloria asked.

"It will also have a telegraph office," Clint said.

"So?" Jennalee asked.

"Gloria told me you girls stole this wagon," Clint said. "Carthage might use that against you. Also, word might have gotten out about what happened in Cotswold. There won't be any way to hide the six of you in this town."

"Are you saying that we shouldn't go in?" Jennalee asked.

"I could ride in, buy the supplies, and then meet you somewhere."

The women all exchanged a glance.

"So we should give you our money to buy supplies and just let you ride off?" Jennalee asked.

"Jen—" Gloria said.

"No," Clint said, "Jennalee's right. There's no reason

47

why any of you should trust me with your money. One or two of you should come with me.''

"One or two of us wouldn't be able to keep you from taking off with the money,'' Rachel said, showing that it wasn't only Jennalee who was worried.

"All right, then,'' Clint said. "Two of you take the wagon into town and buy the supplies. I'll wait here with the rest.''

The women all began to exchange glances.

"Okay, Gloria, Jennalee,'' Rachel said, "here's where you can start telling us what to do.''

"I think two of us should go in with Clint,'' Gloria said.

"I'll go,'' Jennalee said.

"A black woman and a white man?'' Kathy asked.

"A black woman,'' Jennalee said, "a white woman and a white man. Everybody will just assume that I'm a servant girl.''

"Okay,'' Gloria said, "why don't you and Rachel go with Clint. The rest of us will camp near here and wait.''

"We'll take the wagon,'' Clint said. "We can fill it with supplies.''

"Agreed?'' Gloria asked.

They all agreed, and went to look for a spot to make camp and wait.

Clint decided to leave Duke behind. The big gelding was too easily recognizable. He would ride in the wagon with Jennalee and Rachel. It had been a long time since he'd driven his own gunsmithing rig, which he'd left behind more often than not in Labyrinth these days. It just took too long to travel around that way.

He also took Gloria aside before leaving and handed her his Colt New Line. . . .

"Can you use this?''

"Yes.''

"Good,'' he said. "Keep it on you, in the pocket of your

skirt, or in your belt, or just hold it in your hand, but keep it with you at all times, understand?''

"Yes, I understand.''

"And don't be afraid to use it,'' Clint said. "A group of women alone can be forgiven almost any shooting.''

"I'm not going to shoot anyone unless I have to,'' she said.

"That's a good attitude to take,'' he said, "but when that time does come, don't hesitate. More people get killed because they hesitate.''

"All right.''

"Can any of the others shoot?'' he asked. "I can leave my rifle.''

"Jennalee can,'' she said, "but she's going with you. None of the others can.''

"Then a rifle would be more of a danger than a help,'' he said. "Just you keep that close, okay?''

"All right,'' she said. "I understand.''

"Good. We'll be back as soon as we can.''

He climbed aboard the wagon with Rachel and Jennalee and started off.

Athens was a bust town, and that was good. Nothing unusual about a wagon driving down the main street. And Jennalee was right. They wouldn't even attract attention because she was along, not as long as Rachel and Clint looked like a couple.

"Can you act married to me?'' Clint asked Rachel as they approached the town.

"Sure,'' she said, and slipped her arm through his, holding his arm with her other hand. "How's this?'' She pressed her hip tightly up against his, too.

"That's fine,'' he said, feeling the heat of her body through her clothes.

Behind them, in the back of the wagon, Jennalee raised her eyebrows.

•   •   •

They rode into town and right up to the general store. Clint reined in the team and put on the brake.

"Rachel, you have the money, right?"

"Right."

"You and Jennalee do the shopping here."

"Where are you going?"

"I'm going to find a gun shop," Clint said. "We can use a couple of extra guns."

"What for?" Jennalee asked.

"So I can teach all of you how to shoot."

"I can shoot just fine," Jennalee said.

"Okay, but the others can't," Clint said, "and you can't all shoot the same gun." He looked at Rachel. "Will you be all right?"

"I'll be fine, dear."

Jennalee frowned and said, "We'll be just fine."

Clint got down and helped the two women down.

"You'd better kiss me before you go off," Rachel said, holding on to his arms as he lowered her to the ground. "You said you wanted us to look married."

"Well, I did, didn't I."

He bent his head to kiss her shortly, but she threw her arms around his neck and kissed him soundly. He couldn't very well pull away—how happily married would that look?—so he decided to kiss her back. He put his arms around her and met her ardor with his own. Her tongue flicked across his lips and teeth before they broke the kiss. Her eyes were shining and she was breathless, and he had an erection that she was very conscious of, since they were pressed tightly together.

"Well," she said, "I've been wanting to do that since I first saw you."

Rachel had red hair and pale skin with freckles across the bridge of her nose. She was a pretty woman, and her mouth was wide and—he knew now—very kissable.

"And?"

"Oh," she said with a big, beautiful smile, "it was even nicer than I thought it would be."

Jennalee leaned closer to them and said to Rachel, "Can we go now . . . ma'am?"

"Of course, Jenny," Rachel said, releasing Clint and looking at her black "servant" girl. "Come along, Jenny. We'll see you later, Clint, dear."

"See you later . . . Rachel, uh, dear."

He turned away, still able to taste her on his lips—and thoroughly liking it.

TWELVE

Clint bought two Paterson Colts he thought the women would be able to handle. He didn't know if they didn't shoot well, or if some of them had never fired a gun at all, but there was no point in taking a chance. A beginner trying to fire a full-sized Colt could end up with a broken wrist.

He had the clerk wrap them in brown paper so no one would know what he was carrying, and then he left the shop and walked back to the general store.

Before he even got there he knew there was trouble.

There were three men in the general store when Rachel and Jennalee entered, and they not only took a shine to the white girl, but the black one, as well.

"Look at that black gal," one of them said to his friends. "Mmm, mmmm, I got to get me some dark meat today. Them tits is some of the nicest eatin' I ever did see."

"Look at the white one," the other man said, "and that red hair. And *her* body would make some fine eatin'."

"You fellas better get over to the whorehouse quick," the third man said.

"Whorehouse nothin'," the first man said, "I see what I want right here."

"Can I help you?" the clerk asked Rachel.

"Yes," she said, "my husband will be back any minute, and we need some supplies. I have a list."

"Well, ma'am, you just let me have it and we'll see if we can fill it for you. Um, is the darky with you, ma'am?" the clerk asked.

"Why, yes," Rachel said, "she's my . . . servant."

"I see. Well, then, she can help me collect some of the supplies."

"Of course," Rachel said. "Jenny, help the man."

"Now's my chance," the first man said. His name was Leo, and he was convinced there wasn't a woman alive who didn't want him.

"Leo," his friend Vince said, "you heard what she said about her husband."

"Who's afraid of some farmer," Leo said. "Leave go of my arm, Vince."

While Vince watched Leo walk over to Rachel, the other man, Dean, began to stalk Jenny around the store. He was behind her when she reached up to get something from a top shelf. The fabric of her dress pulled taut across her high buttocks. Dean couldn't control himself, then, and he slid his hands up her skirt from behind to get a feel of her fine, black flesh.

"Hey!" she snapped. She turned and looked into his grinning face. She closed her fist and punched him squarely in the nose. It exploded in a shower of red and he staggered back, clamping his hands over it to staunch the flow of blood.

"Don't even touch me!" Jennalee shouted.

"Aw, hell," the clerk said, "aw, ma'am, can't you control your darky? She can't be hitting my customers."

"He put his hands under my dress," Jennalee said.

"You heard her," Rachel said. "What kind of customers you got here?"

"Ma'am," Leo said, removing his hat, "I'd like to apologize for my friend. Maybe you and me could go over to the hotel and get a room—"

"I don't think so," Rachel said, giving him a disgusted look. "Let me pass." She wanted to go and stand with Jennalee.

"She bwoke my dose," Dean said from behind his hands. "Goddamn nigger bitch!"

He moved one hand away from his face to draw his gun. His hand was so slick with blood, though, that it slipped from his fingers and fell to the floor. Before he could recover it, Jennalee picked it up, backed away, and pointed it at him.

"Black bitch!" he said, spitting blood in a spray. He took a step toward her, and she cocked the hammer on the gun.

"One more step and you're a dead man," she said. "I don't let the likes of you put his hands on me without my permission."

"Now, little lady," Vince said, his hand hovering over his own gun, "I can't let you shoot him, so why don't you put the gun down."

"You get him to back away," Jennalee said.

"Ma'am, can't you control your darky?" the clerk pleaded.

"Let go of me!" Rachel shouted at Leo, who had her by the arm.

"The hotel's right across the street," he said soothingly. "Come on, you know you want to."

"Put the gun down, lady," Vince said again, "I'm beggin' ya."

"Get your friend out of here."

"Shoot her, Vince," Dean cried out.

"I'm gettin' the sheriff," the clerk said, and rushed toward the door.

They were all so busy that none of them noticed Clint enter the store and take the whole picture in very quickly. The clerk slipped past him out of the store.

"Dear," he said to Rachel, "is there a problem?"

THIRTEEN

"That's my wife you've got by the arm, friend," Clint said to Leo. "I'd advise you to let her go."

"Your wife?" Leo asked. He was expecting a fat farmer.

"That's right."

Leo let go of her arm, and Rachel ran over to stand next to Jennalee.

"We was just havin' some fun, mister," Leo said.

"Yeah," Clint said, "I can see that by your friend's face."

"Mister," Vince said, "if this darky is yours, you better get her to put that gun down."

"Whose is it?"

"My partner's."

"The one with the bloody nose?"

"That's right."

"And what was he going to do with it?"

"I was gonna shoot the bitch!" Dean said. "She bwoke my dose."

"She punched him," Vince said.

"And what did he do to deserve it?"

"He put his hands under Jenny's skirt," Rachel said.

"Well," Clint said, looking at Vince, "if he did that I think she's entitled to shoot him."

"Mister—" Vince said, his hand still hovering over his gun.

"On the other hand," Clint said to Vince, "if you go for that gun, I'll kill you."

Vince's eyes widened.

"Over some nigger gal?"

"Over a woman," Clint said. "Get your friend out of here and get him to a doc—I can see you, too, friend," Clint said to Leo. "I think you boys had better take your guns out with your fingertips and drop them on the floor—now!"

"We're two to your one, mister," Vince told him.

"Well," Clint said, "you're free to go for your guns at any time, but I'm warning you, I'll kill both of you, and she'll kill your friend with the bloody nose."

"He's unarmed!" Vince said.

"Well, she gets nervous around guns, don't you, Jenny?" Clint asked.

"Real nervous," she said. Judging from the smile on her face, she was starting to have a good time.

"So do like I say," Clint said, "and all three of you get to walk out of here."

"Without our guns?" Leo asked.

"That's right."

"We'll be a laughingstock."

"You boys will be alive," a new voice said, coming from the door behind Clint.

"Sheriff," Leo said, "these folks—"

"I can see what's goin' on, Leo," the man said. "I think I should introduce you to this gentleman, here. His name is Clint Adams."

"Clint . . ." Vince said.

". . . Adams?" Leo asked.

"That's right."

"The . . . Gunsmith?" Vince asked.

"Do like the man said, boys," the sheriff said. "Guns on the floor."

Clint had made a half turn so he could include the sheriff in his line of vision.

"Just take it easy, Mr. Adams," the man said. "Let's try and get this settled without any gunfire."

"I'd like that, Sheriff," Clint said. "We just came to town for some supplies. Once we get them we'll be on our way again."

"The two women are with you?" the lawman asked.

"That's right."

"Can you get the lady with the gun to lower it?"

"Jenny?"

Reluctantly, Jenny did.

"Boys? Guns on the floor, if you want to live."

Both men had frozen when they were struck by the enormity of what they had been about to do: draw on the Gunsmith! Suddenly, they withdrew their weapons with their fingertips and dropped them to the floor.

"Now get Dean over to the doc."

They cautiously collected their still bleeding friend and helped him out the door.

Clint walked over to Jenny and took the gun from her. When he saw it was sticky with blood he simply let it drop to the floor, then turned.

"Much obliged for the help, Sheriff," he said.

"The name's Cates," the man said, "and I'm sorry those boys were botherin' your womenfolk. Frank, the clerk, he came and got me, and I managed to get the full story out of him." He turned to the women. "Ladies, I'm sorry this happened. Why don't you collect your supplies and take them to the wagon."

Most of the supplies they'd ordered were on the counter, except for what Jennalee had been reaching for. She turned and reached for it now, and Clint and the sheriff both found themselves looking at her ass while she did it.

"Clint!" Rachel said.

"Rachel," he replied, embarrassed at having been caught

looking, and maybe even sympathizing with poor Dean a little bit.

"Can you help me?"

"Sure."

Clint went and collected some of the supplies and took them outside.

Rachel looked at the sheriff, who was in his thirties and eyeing her with open appreciation.

"I need to pay for these things," she said.

"Sure," he said. "I'll get Frank."

Outside the sheriff ran into Clint and said, "You got to appreciate that the boys don't get to be around good-looking women like these—"

"No excuse for bad manners, Sheriff."

"Yeah," the man said, "I know. I'll go get Frank so you can pay him. He's, uh, waiting in my office."

"Much obliged."

Clint went inside.

"I'm glad you came along when you did," Jenny said. "I was gonna shoot that man."

"How'd you break his nose?"

"With my fist," she said, and showed it to him. "I don't like having my ass pawed without my say-so."

"Can't say I blame you for that," Clint said. "When that clerk gets back let's pay for our supplies and get out of town before those boys come back with some friends."

"I don't think they'll be back," Rachel said. "They know who you are now."

"And if they know, so do others," Clint said, "and that just might bring more trouble, not serve to avoid it."

"I see what you mean," Rachel said.

The clerk entered the store nervously, and Rachel began to count out the money.

"Does that cover it?" she asked, shoving it into his hands.

"That's fine, ma'am," the clerk said, eyeing Clint with open fear. "That's fine."

The clerk knew who he was, and so did those cowhands, and the sheriff, and pretty soon so would the whole town.

"Let's get out of here," he said to the women.

FOURTEEN

When they got back to the camp they told the other girls everything that had happened.

"You called Rachel 'ma'am'?" Ally asked.

"Is that all you heard?" Jennalee asked.

"But no one was hurt, right?" Gloria asked.

"That's right," Clint said, removing some of the supplies from the wagon. They were going to have to be redistributed so there'd still be room for everyone to ride in the back. Also, they'd need some for that night's meal.

"So what's the problem?" Gloria asked.

Clint handed Kathy some coffee so she could start a pot, then turned to face Gloria.

"The standoff in the store," he said, "is the kind of thing that gets around."

"Well, what about you killing three men in the street?" she asked. "That gets around, too."

"We'd already left that behind," he explained. "This is new. This pinpoints our location, gives somebody a new starting point to look for us from."

"Somebody meaning Ted Carthage."

"Or Ben Swallow," Clint said. "If he's half as good a tracker as his reputation says, that's all he would need."

"So what do we do?" she asked. "Not go to California?"

"We already agreed," Jennalee said, "we're going to San Francisco."

"We can still go," Clint said, "we just might have to take a more . . . indirect route."

"How indirect?" Jennalee asked.

"I'll have to think about it."

"If only this hadn't happened," Gloria said.

"It wasn't my fault," the black girl said. "That man put his hands on my butt."

"How many sets of hands have you had on your butt, Jenny?" Rachel asked.

"Not as many as you," Jennalee said, facing Rachel angrily. "And you were just a little too comfortable with ordering me around, missy."

"Jennalee's right," Clint said, getting between them. "It wasn't her fault. That man had no right to do what he did."

Jennalee looked at him and said, "Thank you."

"And maybe this won't get written up," Clint said. "After all, like you said, Gloria, nobody was hurt."

Ed Willis was excited. He'd been the editor of the *Athens Democrat* for eight years and nothing exciting had ever happened before. Now he had the Gunsmith to write about.

This was going to be his best front page ever.

FIFTEEN

They remained camped where they were and Clint took time to rearrange the supplies in the back of the wagon. By the time he was done, the women had supper ready and he sat by the fire and ate. He was surprised when Jennalee came over and sat next to him, handing him a cup of coffee.

"I didn't get a chance to really say thank you," she said.

"That's okay."

"No," she said, "I mean for what you did in town, and also for siding with me later. It really wasn't my fault."

"I know."

She looked straight ahead and said, "I really wanted to shoot that man, but Rachel's right. I've had so many men's hands on my butt, I don't know why I got so mad."

"I think you were entitled to get mad."

She smiled, mostly without humor, and asked, "Are you just tryin' to get on my good side?"

"No," he said, "I really agree with you, Jennalee."

"Well," she said, "if that's the case, you can just start calling me Jenny from now on."

"And you'll start calling me Clint?" he asked. "Instead of 'that white man'?"

Now she smiled for real, and it reached her eyes.

"All right," she said. "That's a deal."

She got up and walked away, but she was only gone a minute before Rachel reappeared.

"I have to talk to you," she said.

"All right," he said. "Talk."

"Not here."

"Is it about what happened today?"

"Partly," she said, "but not here. Later go for a walk. I found a clearing about a hundred yards from here. Meet me there, inside a circle of brush."

"You just happened to stumble across this circle of brush?"

"I went for a walk."

"You shouldn't be wandering from camp, Rachel."

"Just meet me there," she said, "and scold me later."

Before he could say anything she got up and walked away. Several minutes later Gloria came over and sat. He was very popular tonight.

"Have you thought about what we should do?" she asked.

"Maybe I'm just being too careful," he said.

"I didn't think you could be too careful."

"Well, we'll just take a circular route before we head in a straight line to San Francisco," he said. "Might add half a day to the trip."

"All right."

"And if we wanted to be real careful . . ." he said.

"What?"

"We'd get rid of this wagon and find another," he said.

"Why?"

"So we can leave a different set of tracks," he told her. "And don't forget, this one is stolen."

"Oh, yeah . . ."

For a moment she looked as if there was something she wanted to tell him, but she didn't say anything.

"Clint, Miriam wants to come over and sit by you," she said instead. "Is that all right?"

"It's fine with me, Gloria, if you think it's wise," he replied.

"Oh, I don't think it will be a problem," she said. "Just talk to her, she's feeling a little frightened by all this."

"Okay," Clint said, "send her over—and why don't you have her bring me another cup of coffee, too." He handed her the empty cup.

"She'll be thrilled."

Clint watched Gloria walk across the camp to where Miriam was sitting and give her the news. You would have thought someone told the young girl she'd won a bundle of money. She bounced up, took the empty cup from Gloria, and hurried to the campfire to fill it. Then she carried it over to Clint. The closer she got, however, the slower her step became and by the time she reached him, instead of looking happy, she looked both shy and scared.

"H-here's your coffee, Clint."

"Thank you, Miriam," he said, taking it from her. "Why don't you sit and talk awhile?"

"Oh," she said, seemingly flustered by the invitation, "I don't want to bother you . . ."

"You're not bothering me," he said. "I could use the company."

"Well," she said, gathering her skirts, "all right," and she sat beside him. "I don't really think you need the company, though."

"Why's that?"

"I see all the girls coming over to sit with you," she said.

"Well," he said, "I am the only man here, and you've only got each other to talk to if you don't talk to me. So now it's your turn."

"I suppose . . ."

They talked for a while, mostly Clint asking her questions and she answering them. She had come from the East and she was very excited when he told her that he had also come west from there, though many years ago.

Mostly he just listened to her talk, and it seemed to calm her. Finally, she started to actually talk about being scared.

"There's nothing wrong with being scared, Miriam," he said.

"I guess not. . . . I just seem to be scared all the time."

"You mean since you left Carthage?"

"No," she said, "*all* the time. While I was there I was always afraid that one of those men was gonna kill me. They . . . were very rough."

"Well," he said, "you don't have to worry about that anymore."

"B-but they found us," she said. "When that man was dragging me through the street, and I was . . . well, exposed, I thought he was going to kill me. He might have, if you hadn't come along."

He reached out and touched her arm.

"Miriam, I'm not going to let anyone hurt you or kill you. I promise."

"This is the only time I've ever felt safe," she confided, "I mean, since you came along. I can't thank you enough. I can't tell you—"

She stopped abruptly, looked as if she was close to tears, and then ran off.

Just for that moment he didn't know if he'd made things better or worse.

SIXTEEN

Clint told Gloria he was going to take a walk before turning in.

"We've divvied up the watches among us tonight so you can sleep," she told him. "Since you're the only one who knows the way to San Francisco, we figured you should be nice and rested when we start out."

"That's real considerate of you girls," Clint said. "Thanks."

He walked out of camp and headed north, the direction Rachel had given him. Before long he came to a clearing, and in the center of the clearing was a stand of brush. It looked dense to him, but he approached it and parted it with his hands. To his amazement it was hollow inside, and Rachel was there waiting for him. He stepped through the brush and it closed behind him. He looked up and could see the sky, and the moon was full and bright. He felt as if he was in a cabin with no roof on top.

"How did you ever find this place?" he asked her.

"I was looking for someplace special," she said.

"For what?"

"For this," she said, and suddenly her dress was down around her ankles. The moonlight illuminated her and cast

69

shadows so that she was all curves and dark, mysterious places.

"Rachel—"

"We're supposed to act married, remember?"

"That was in town."

"When we kissed," she said, "you're not gonna tell me you didn't feel anything, are you?"

"Well, no, of course not—"

"Because," she said, moving closer to him, "I sure felt something between us." Her hand came up to touch him, and then cup him. "And there it is again."

"Rachel—"

"Come on, Clint," she whispered, pressing herself up against him. Her breasts were large and firm, her skin fragrant, and there was another odor, a musty odor of her readiness. "You're gonna be around six women for a long time, your balls are gonna get blue if we don't do something about it—like this!"

She got down on her knees and he saw, for the first time, that she'd brought a couple of blankets and spread them on the ground. The little minx had this all planned.

She closed her mouth on him right through his trousers, and he could feel the heat of her mouth. Quickly she undid his pants and, rather than fight her, he unbuckled his gun belt and slung it over his shoulder, unsure what to do with it. With that out of the way she was able to yank down his trousers and shorts, and his penis jutted out at full attention, rigid and red.

"Um," she said, and took it into her mouth. She sucked him avidly and he had to spread his legs to keep his balance. She slid her hands up the backs of his thighs and then cupped his butt cheeks firmly. As she sucked him she pulled him to her, taking the full length of him down her throat. Clint wondered if each of the whores had her specialty and this was Rachel's. She sure did it well enough for it to be her specialty.

When his legs began to tremble, signaling that his orgasm was near, she released him. Glossy with her saliva, his penis felt cold in the night air.

"I know, darling," she said, "you're chilled, but I have a warm, wet place for you."

She sat down on the blanket, then lay down on her back, holding her legs open for him. In fact, she gripped her ankles and held herself wide open for him. Instead of kneeling between her legs and driving himself into her, he bent over and began to lick her. She gasped and released her ankles in surprise so that her heels came down on his back, but he didn't seem to notice. He was busily eating her, licking and sucking and forgetting where they were, or that some yards away there was a camp with five other women in it. She got noisy, then, as his tongue found her clit and it wouldn't be until later that he wondered if anyone had heard them. Now all he could hear was the blood pounding in his ears and Rachel's moans and cries as he used his mouth and tongue to bring her to a climax.

Before the waves of pleasure could fade he was on her and in her. She gasped again as he drove his rigid penis into her. There was no give to the ground beneath her, and he entered her all the way, going as deep as he could possibly go. Once again her heels were on his back, drumming this time, and once again he was too busy to notice. He gritted his teeth and started slamming in and out of her as hard as he could. The hard ground must not have been hurting her because she took up a litany of, "Yes, yes, yes," every time he drove back into her.

He drove and drove himself into her until his legs seemed to fill with molten lava, which welled up inside of him and then exploded and he squirted and squirted and squirted into her. . . .

"Isn't the sky beautiful?" she asked moments later. She was still on her back, staring at the stars. He was lying with his head on her shoulder, his mouth close to the nipple of her right breast.

He rolled over so he could look at the sky.

"Yes, it is beautiful," he said, "but I think we'd better get back to camp before we're missed."

"Before we go back," she said, "we have to talk."

"About what?" he asked, getting to his feet and pulling up his shorts and trousers. Amazingly, all the while they'd been having sex his gun belt had not fallen from his shoulder.

"About us."

"What about us?"

"Well, Clint," she said, "there are six women on this trip. Clearly you have to make a choice."

"And you think it should be you?"

She smiled and stretched her arms up over her head, lifting her breasts, extending her lush body. Except for Gloria, Rachel had the fullest body of all the women.

"You're here, aren't you?"

"I didn't know what you wanted when I came out here, Rachel."

"Didn't you?"

"No—and I think in the interest of having everyone get along, none of the other girls should know what we did."

"They'd be jealous."

"I'm sure that would give you satisfaction," he said, "but it would do nothing for the general mood during the trip. We all have to be able to rely on each other, Rachel, and we can't do that if there's animosity."

"Well," she said, sitting up and wrapping her arms around her knees, "it doesn't matter what happens after this, or who you sleep with, I was the first."

He didn't say anything.

"Wasn't I?"

"I think you'd better get dressed and come back to camp, Rachel," he said, and slipped through the brush, leaving her alone inside. He was smiling as he walked back to camp.

SEVENTEEN

When Clint got back to camp he had the feeling everyone was watching him. As a man who lived by the gun he could almost always tell when a man had recently been in a gun-fight. The smell of a gun battle was always on a man's clothes. He wondered if it was the same with prostitutes. Could they smell Rachel on him?

He watched carefully when Rachel returned to camp, every hair in place, looking very demure—as demure as a whore could look. It didn't seem to him that the other women paid any special attention to her. Maybe he was imagining it when he came back. Maybe it was just his guilt at not being able to turn Rachel down. However, he felt it would have been the same no matter who the woman was. If any of these gals had been waiting for him, and had dropped her dress, the results would have been the same.

After all, he *was* a man.

Clint went to the fire and poured himself a cup of coffee. He listened while the women divvied up the watches for the night. At one point he caught Rachel looking over at him, and he looked away, wondering if any of the other women had caught the moment.

Guilt was a terrible thing.

• • •

In the morning they woke him and he was again impressed at how organized the women were. Before long they had broken camp, doused the campfire, and had the wagon ready to go. Clint saddled Duke and mounted up.

"California or bust," Gloria said, as they prepared to leave. She looked at Clint and asked, "Which way?"

Clint pointed west and said, "Follow me."

For most of that day Clint kept an eye ahead and an eye behind. It was the first time he had ever traveled with six wanted women, even though they weren't wanted by the law. Even if Carthage had accused them of stealing his wagon, that wouldn't have been enough to put out a wanted poster. So they didn't have to worry about the law being after them, just Ben Swallow and his men—which was bad enough.

Clint had heard for years of Swallow and his men, but had never crossed trails with them. It seemed inevitable now, and would probably happen under the worst of circumstances.

He tried to remember how many men Swallow had.

EIGHTEEN

Ben Swallow rode into Athens with six of his men. They had met him with a horse at the nearest railhead, and they'd gone straight from there to town.

"Spread out," Swallow said as they rode into Athens. "I doubt they're still here, but it's possible."

"What are you gonna do, Ben?" Ab Nevers asked.

"I'll check with the sheriff," Swallow said. "If Adams was here he'll know. The rest of you fan out. Ab? You're with me."

"Sure, Ben."

Ab Nevers was Swallow's right-hand man and had been for the past eight months, since the death of Winston Bates. Bates had filled that position for eight years before succumbing to the same disease that Doc Holliday suffered from. For the last year of his life Bates had been preparing Nevers to fill his shoes. It didn't seem to matter that Nevers, at twenty-eight, was the youngest of Swallow's men. He'd been with them for three years, most of those spent in the company of Bates. He was smart and steady, and that was what Swallow needed in his foreman.

Together they rode to the sheriff's office, but before they could even enter Nevers spotted something and called Swallow's attention to it.

"Ben? Look at this paper."

Nevers handed Swallow a copy of the *Athens Democrat*, which had been sitting on a bench outside the office. The headline read, GUNSMITH BACKS DOWN THREE MEN IN ATHENS GENERAL STORE.

"I told you," Swallow said to Nevers. "I told you they were heading this way."

"I know you told me," Ab Nevers said, "but how did you know? *That* you never tell me."

"That can't be taught, boy," Swallow said, folding up the newspaper and putting it in his jacket pocket. "That you just got to come by."

They entered the office.

Sheriff Web Cates looked up as the two men entered his office. From the look of them they had just ridden a ways, and more than that, they looked like they did a lot of riding.

"Sheriff?" the older one said.

"That's right," the lawman said. "Web Cates. And you'd be Ben Swallow."

Swallow stopped short in front of the sheriff's desk.

"You know me?"

"I've seen you once or twice."

"I've never been here before."

Cates smiled.

"I wasn't always the sheriff of Athens, Mr. Swallow. What can I do for you?"

"This is my foreman, Ab Nevers."

Cates and Nevers nodded to each other.

"We're looking for someone," Swallow said.

"Why doesn't that surprise me?" Cates asked. "Who you lookin' for?"

"Well, actually we're looking for six women."

"Women?" Cates asked. "You're trackin' women?"

"That's right."

"What'd they do?"

"Took somethin' that didn't belong to them," Swallow said. "Me and my boys are gonna get it back."

"Well," Cates said, shaking his head, "if six desperate women had passed through my town I think I'd know about it."

"Well, from what we understand they're travelin' with someone."

"Oh? Who might that be?"

Swallow took the newspaper from his pocket and held it out so the lawman could see the headline.

"Clint Adams?" Cates asked.

"That's right."

"Wait a minute," the sheriff said. "Was one of them women black?"

"That's right."

"And a red-haired gal?"

"Right again."

"He said they were married. I mean, him and the red-haired gal."

"Well, they're not," Swallow said.

"But there wasn't six women with him," Cates said, "just two."

"He probably left the other four outside of town so they wouldn't attract attention."

"Well, I guess he should have stayed out of town if he didn't want to attract any attention," Cates said. "Did you read that story?"

"The headline tells it all, I'll bet."

"Three of our locals took a shine to those two women," Cates said, "and Adams had to back them down when things got rough."

"Like I said," Swallow repeated, dropping the slim newspaper on the man's desk, "the headline tells it all."

"Well, that was two or three days ago," Cates said, picking up the paper. "Yeah, here it is, you missed them by three days."

"We've been closer than that and something always seems to go wrong."

"Well, looks like something's really gone wrong now if they've hooked up with the Gunsmith."

"I've got six good men with me, Sheriff," Swallow said. "I think we can handle one man."

"Well, this one man's making the news lately. Backed three men down here in Athens, and I heard tell he gunned three men down a while back. Wouldn't have been your men, would they?"

"They were," Swallow said, "but they didn't know who they were dealing with. We do now."

"Well," Cates said dubiously, "I guess that can make a difference."

"You talk to Adams while he was here, Sheriff?"

"Briefly," Cates said. "I saw him back those three down, but I had to make sure they'd stay backed down. We talked."

"Any idea where they were headed?"

"We didn't talk that much. They pretty much stopped into the general store, picked up some supplies, and left. It was a pretty short visit."

"Maybe long enough," Swallow said. "I'll be able to tell how far they plan on going by how much they bought in the way of supplies."

"What if they're just buying supplies from town to town?"

"That ain't what you do when you're on the run," Ab Nevers said, speaking for the first time. "You wanna stock up, because you want to make as few stops as possible."

Swallow gave Nevers a look a proud father gives to a son who's learned his lessons well.

"Well," Cates said grudgingly. "I guess that makes sense."

"Yes, it does," Swallow said. "Much obliged for your time, Sheriff."

"Uh, how long you boys plan on stayin' in town?" Cates asked.

At the door Swallow said, "Just long enough to get the information we need. Don't worry, Sheriff, ours will be a short visit, too."

NINETEEN

"Try it again," Clint said to Miriam.

"I hate to disappoint you," she said.

"You're not disappointing me, Miriam," Clint assured her. "Just hold the gun in both hands, point it, and squeeze the trigger. *Pull* the trigger, don't jerk it. That's what's making your shot go wild."

The other five women watched as Clint gave Miriam her shooting lesson. Each of them had fired the gun, and only Jenny had hit the target—a big, wide tree that would be almost impossible to miss for anyone who had ever fired a handgun before. Unfortunately, none of them—except for Jenny—had.

But he had finally succeeded in getting the others to squeeze the trigger. It was taking a little longer with Miriam.

"She ain't gonna do it," Jenny said.

"Sure she is," Gloria said.

"No, she's not," Rachel said. "She's too scared."

"All right," Clint said. "Now point and squeeze."

Miriam had the pointing part down just right, but when she tried to squeeze the trigger all of a sudden her hands went up, and she fired into the air.

"Miriam—" Clint said.

"I'm sorry, I'm so sorry—"

"Calm down," Clint said. "Tell me why you keep jerking your hands up in the air."

"Well," the young woman said, "I try to squeeze the trigger, like you say, but I know when I do it's gonna make a loud noise, and I don't like the noise so I just . . . flinch."

Clint thought it was more of a jerk than a flinch, but he didn't say anything.

"Why don't we stop for today," Clint said, taking the gun away from her, "and we'll take it up again tomorrow."

"All right," Miriam said. "I'm terribly sorry to disappoint you, Clint."

Clint put his arm around her shoulders and said, "Miriam, you're not disappointing me, so stop worrying about that, all right?"

"A-all right," she said. "You're so kind."

Gloria came over and said, "Come, Miriam, it's our turn to cook tonight."

She and Clint exchanged a look over her shoulder and then Gloria led her away. The other girls came over to Clint.

"I'd like to try again," Kathy said. "I think I can hit the target now."

"No, girls," Clint said, "we'll try it again tomorrow."

"Darn," Kathy said and turned away. "Come on, Ally, let's go check the horses."

"The horses are fine," Ally said.

Kathy turned and put her hands on her hips.

"If those horses get away, we're sunk!"

Ally looked at Clint and said, "I don't know why she's always so worried about the horses getting away."

As Ally ran after Kathy, Clint said to Jenny and Rachel, "Maybe that's because they almost did the other night when Kathy forgot to tie them off."

Both women started walking back toward camp with him.

"Jenny, don't you have to do something?" Rachel asked.

"Not right now, Rachel," the black girl said. "How about you?"

"No."

"I just want to talk to Clint about guns," Jenny said.

"Guns," Rachel said. "I hate guns." Seeing that she wasn't going to get Clint alone—and hadn't been able to since that night they'd made love—she said, "Well, I'm sure I can find something to do," and trotted off.

"What do you want to know about guns?" Clint asked.

"Nothing," Jenny said. "I know about guns, Clint Adams. What I want to know is why you had to sleep with Rachel."

"What?"

"Don't deny it," Jenny said. "I can see it when she looks at you. First she was all over you in Athens, and then—did it happen that night? When you both went off for a walk?"

"Well . . . yes."

"I knew it."

"Does anyone else know it?"

"I don't know," Jenny said. "Maybe Gloria, but not the others."

"Unless Rachel's told them."

"She hasn't," Jenny said. "If she had, I'd know about it. Why did it happen?"

"It just did," Clint said. "I went for a walk, and there she was—"

"She told you to meet her, didn't she?" Jenny asked. "And then she dropped her dress."

He gaped at her.

"How did you know that?"

"In case you haven't noticed," Jenny said, "Rachel's a little forward. The girls have been talking about you since we met you. I was just wondering how long it would take Rachel to get around to it."

"Well, it hasn't happened since then."

"It won't take long before the others decide to get forward, too," Jenny said. "Kathy and Ally have already been wondering what it would be like to be with the Gunsmith."

"And you haven't?" he asked.

"Honey," she said, "you just ain't my type."

"I see."

"And it's got nothin' to do with your color," Jenny said hurriedly. "Sure, I don't like most white men, but I also don't like violent men."

"I'm not violent."

"I saw you kill three men."

"That was to save all of you," he said. "And talk about violent? Who was it that punched a man in the nose and took his gun in Athens? I almost had to kill three more men because of that."

"He grabbed my butt," Jenny said.

Before he could stop himself, Clint said, "Can't say I much blame him."

Jenny gave him a look, and for a moment he thought she was going to be offended. Instead, she smiled and said, "Don't you be gettin' any ideas, Mr. Gunsmith. I can still punch."

She walked away, then, and he knew she was adding a little twitch of her hips and butt for him as she did.

TWENTY

Ben Swallow held up his hand to signal to his men to stop.

"This is it," he said. "This is where they camped. He left the other women here while he and the other two went into town. Caleb?"

"Yeah, Ben," one of the men answered.

"Take a look around, tell me what you see."

Caleb Manson was the best sign tracker Swallow ever knew. He could read sign that was almost invisible to the naked eye.

"The rest of you stay mounted until he's done."

They all remained where they were and watched Caleb work his magic on the ground.

"Ben?" Ab Nevers said.

"Yeah."

"Where have you decided they're headed?"

"Someplace they think we'd never look," Swallow said.

"And where's that?"

Swallow looked at his foreman.

"I haven't decided yet. I'm thinking either California or Canada."

"Maybe Alaska, huh?" Nevers asked.

"That, too. With the supplies they bought they plan on traveling a long time."

"What about Mexico?"

"I don't think six whores are gonna want to go to Mexico, Ab," Swallow said. "In fact, the more I think about it, the more I think it's California."

"Why's that?"

"They'd blend in," Swallow said. "Especially a place like San Francisco."

"San Francisco sounds good to me," Nevers said. "I've never been there."

"Well, we're not gonna head there on my say-so," Swallow said. "We'll track 'em awhile and see where they lead us."

Caleb Manson came walking over to Swallow's horse.

"I see seven sets of tracks, Ben. Six women and a man."

"What about horses?"

"Three. One of them is a great big animal. Don't the Gunsmith ride a big gelding?"

"That's right."

"Anything else?" Nevers asked.

"Wagon tracks are deep," Caleb said. "It's loaded down pretty good."

"Okay," Swallow said, "mount up, Caleb. We'll follow the tracks for a while."

"That won't be hard," Caleb said, swinging into his saddle. "That wagon's gonna be easy to follow."

Swallow turned in his saddle and looked at his men.

"Before we get started I want to know if anybody's got a problem with tanglin' with the Gunsmith."

"We're gettin' paid, ain't we?" Dan Yearwood asked.

"You sure are," Ben Swallow said, "double for Clint Adams."

"Then who's got a problem?" Jim Davis asked.

"Besides," Caleb chimed in, "we owe him for takin' three of us out."

Zack Wilson cleared his throat.

"You got somethin' to say, Zack?" Swallow asked.

"I was just wonderin'," Wilson said, "if we might not need some more men?"

"How many more men do you think we need, Zack?" Swallow asked. "Five? Ten? Fifty?"

"Uh, I don't know—"

"I think the seven of us can pretty much handle anybody, don't you?" Swallow asked.

"Al was really good with a gun," Zack said, "and Adams took him and two others—"

"Seven of us, Zack," Ben Swallow said. "Even the Gunsmith wouldn't be foolish enough to try all seven of us at one time. The answer's no, I don't think we need any more men. Okay?"

"Sure, boss," Zack said. "I was just askin'."

"Well, don't ask again," Swallow said, "or I'm liable to think you're not up to this."

"Hey," Zack said, "I never said I was out. I'm with ya all the way."

"Okay, then," Swallow said. "Caleb? Take the point. We're followin' you."

"Got ya, boss," Caleb said. "This is gonna be a piece of cake."

TWENTY-ONE

They were just outside of Gentry, Utah, when the right rear wheel slipped off a rock and broke with an audible crack. Suddenly, the wagon listed to one side and the girls inside shouted. Miriam was sitting in front with Gloria, who was driving, and as the wagon leaned she lost her balance and started to fall. Luckily, Clint was riding right along with them. He reached out and caught her before she could tumble to the ground.

"Thank you," she said, giving him an adoring look.

"That's okay," he said, setting her gently on her feet.

Gloria climbed down and the other girls got out of the back of the wagon. Clint dismounted, and they all stood there and stared at the wheel.

"Can we fix that?" Kathy asked.

"That's a pretty bad break," Clint said. "I don't think so."

"What do we do, then?" Miriam asked.

"I saw a sign about a mile back for Gentry," Clint said. "It's not that far ahead. We were going to bypass it, but I guess I'll have to go in and buy a wheel."

"But we didn't want to have to stop in any more towns," Ally said.

"We don't have much of a choice this time, Ally," Clint said.

"Well," Gloria said. "I think one of us should go with you."

"Still don't trust me with your money?" Clint asked.

"That's not it," Gloria said. "There are some things we girls need that only another girl can buy."

"Oh, I see. Okay, we'll have to make camp here. You girls will have to empty out the wagon while I'm gone so I'll be able to put the wheel on when I get back."

"All right," Gloria said.

"And you'll need to pick who goes with me."

"I'll go!" Rachel said.

"You went last time, Rachel," Gloria said.

"And look at the trouble we got into," Jenny said.

"That was mostly your fault," Rachel said.

"One of them fellas took a shine to you, too, missy," Jenny said.

"Never mind," Gloria said. "Rachel and Jenny can stay here since they went into town last time. I think I should stay with them."

"And I'll stay with you," Miriam said.

"Okay," Gloria said, "that leaves it between Kathy and Ally. You two decide between you."

The two girls walked off to do just that.

"Make it quick," Clint said. "It'll be dark soon, and I don't know this country all that well."

"Will you be able to get back here with the wheel to-night?" Gloria asked.

"I don't know," Clint said. "If we're not back, though, you'll know why. At the very least we'll be back here with it tomorrow morning."

"We have to stay out here alone?" Miriam asked.

"I'll leave the two Colt Patersons," Clint said. "Jenny can hang on to one, and Gloria the other one. You should be okay."

"Kathy's going," Ally said as she and Kathy returned.

"How'd you decide?" Gloria asked.

"I'll tell you later," Ally said.

"How do I go along?" Kathy asked.

"Can you ride?"

"Sure."

"Bareback?"

"Uh, no."

"I can," Ally said.

"We don't have a saddle for one of the other horses," Clint said. "And we'll have to bring both so we can tie the wagon wheel to the other one."

"Then I guess Ally has to go," Kathy said, without pouting. Sometimes Clint was surprised at how well these girls got along. The only tension he ever felt existed between Jenny and Rachel, and he wondered if he was the cause of it.

"All right, then," Clint said, "let's get those horses unhitched and we'll get going."

TWENTY-TWO

Clint hadn't been sure that they'd run into Mormons when they were traveling through Utah, but as they drove down Gentry's main street it became very clear that they were in a Mormon town. Mormons, he knew, believed that a man could have more than one wife, but he didn't know their views on prostitutes. He thought he could pretty much guess, though.

"Who are these people?" Ally asked as they rode in. "They're dressed . . . oddly."

"Actually," Clint said, "we're the ones who are going to look odd to them, Ally. They're Mormons."

"Mormons!" Her eyes grew wide, as if Clint had said that the people were Apaches. "I've heard of them, but never seen any of them."

"Well, they're just like you and me," Clint said, "in many ways, and in many ways they're not."

"How wonderful," she said, eyes shining. "I love meeting new people."

"Well," Clint said, "these are new people, all right."

Clint wasn't at all sure how the Mormons would react to the fact that Ally was a whore—or to the fact that there were six of them practically in their midst. They drew curious looks as they rode down the main street, the man on

91

the big gelding, the girl riding bareback, leading a third horse. Ally was going to have to be careful what she said, but they met up with someone before he could talk to her about it.

"Welcome, strangers," a man said, suddenly appearing in front of them. Clint had to rein in Duke to avoid running over the man.

"Hello."

The man was tall, with lots of gray hair and a gray beard. He was wearing coveralls and looked like a farmer.

"Can I help you find something, stranger?" he asked.

"Uh, well, we had an accident outside of your town and broke a wheel on our wagon. We need to buy a new one."

"Ah, well, then you want to go to the end of town," the man said, pointing in the direction they were already going, "to the livery stable. Our man Aaron will be able to help you."

"Aaron," Clint said. "Thank you."

"And the lady?" the man asked. "She is your wife?"

"Well," Clint said, "she's a little young—"

"Yes, sir," she said, "I am his wife, and very happy about it, too."

"And well you should be," the man said. "Marriage is very sacred."

"Oh, I know," Ally said, "I surely do."

"Well, I will not detain you any longer," the man said, and stepped aside.

"Thank you for your help, good sir," Ally said.

"It was my pleasure, young lady, my pleasure," the man said. "We always want to help strangers new to our town."

The man walked off, and Clint and Ally continued down the street.

"For someone who never saw a Mormon before," Clint said to her, "you sure do know how to talk to them."

"He's a man," she said, "and I know how to talk to men."

•   •   •

The man called Aaron was as helpful as the man in the street had been.

"I do have a wheel. What kind of wagon is it?"

"Conestoga," Clint said.

Aaron nodded.

"Yes, it will fit."

"Fine," Clint said. "Then we only have to settle on a price."

"Are you above a little haggling?" Aaron asked.

He was not old, and not young, yet his age was difficult to guess. He seemed very happy to see two strangers in town, and Clint had the feeling that he wanted to haggle only to spend some time talking.

"No, I'm not above haggling."

"Over some food, then?" he asked. "My wife Hannah is a wonderful cook, and you would not be able to get the wheel back to your wagon before nightfall."

Clint looked at Ally, who said nothing and made no gesture. She was leaving the decision entirely up to him.

"I mean both of you, of course," Aaron pressed on. "Please, be my guests for dinner."

"It would be our pleasure, Aaron," Clint said. "Thank you."

"Go to the hotel, tell them I sent you," Aaron said. "I would have you stay with us, but alas, I have no room for guests." He lowered his voice. "With five wives and many little ones running around . . . well, you understand."

"Five wives?" Ally asked.

Aaron misunderstood her, misread her shock.

"Well," he said, "I have my eye on a sixth, you know, but these things take time."

Clint nudged Ally, to keep her from saying anything further.

"Just tell us what time to be there, Aaron," he said.

"Seven," Aaron said. "Seven sharp. That is when we serve dinner."

TWENTY-THREE

"That man has five wives?" Ally said when they got outside.

"It's legal with them, Ally."

"I'm not thinking about legal," she said, shaking her head. "And they think we're disgusting? How can those women put up with that?"

"It's what they were brought up with, I guess," Clint said. "You can't judge them for that."

"And what if they found out what I do for a living?" she asked. "Would they judge me? Would they be inviting me to their house for dinner?"

"Maybe not," Clint said. "What's your point?"

"I just don't understand . . . five wives!"

"Don't condemn it because you don't understand it," Clint said. "Look at it this way. You'll get to see something real unusual tonight."

"I'll say."

When they got to the hotel they took one room, signing in as man and wife. Clint regarded the clerk curiously. The man did not seem as if he was a Mormon.

"I'm not," the clerk said, as if reading his mind.

"Not what?" Clint asked.

"I'm not a Mormon," he said. "You could tell from looking at me that I wasn't."

"Well—"

"Just as I can tell from looking at the two of you that you're not married."

Ally gave Clint a worried look.

"Don't worry," the clerk said. "I live here because it's quiet and peaceful, but every once in a while I have to do something—well, a little daring." He handed Clint the key. "This is it. Have a nice stay."

Up in their room Ally said, "So everyone here isn't Mormon."

"I guess not," Clint said, looking out the window, "but it sure looks like they're the majority."

When he turned Ally was looking in the mirror.

"My God," she said. "I look awful. I can't go to that man's house. I'm covered with dust, and I smell like a horse, and look at this dress—"

Clint crossed the room and grabbed her by the hand.

"Come on," he said, pulling her toward the door.

"Where are we going?"

"To get you a bath and a new dress."

"I can't believe it."

It was an hour later and Ally was once again standing in front of the mirror. This time she smelled clean and fresh, her hair had been washed, and she was wearing a simple but pretty dress.

"This is the nicest dress I've ever had," she said. "I mean, I've had some pretty gowns and frilly things, but this is just the nicest . . . well, regular dress."

"It looks good on you, too."

Clint had also bathed and had purchased a new shirt for dinner.

Ally turned to face him and asked, "How do you want me to play this?"

"What do you mean?"

"I mean do you want a playful wife, an affectionate wife, proper wife—"

"Respectful," he said. "I want a wife who will respect me and our hosts."

"I can do that," she said, turning back to the mirror. "I can be respectful."

"Good," he said.

"Don't worry," she added, "I won't embarrass you."

He smiled and said, "I never thought you would."

TWENTY-FOUR

They walked from the hotel to the house, following Aaron's directions. Along the way they accepted and returned the greetings and good wishes of the people they passed on the street.

"Everyone here is so nice," Ally said, shaking her head.

"It's just the way they are."

"But what do they get out of it?"

Clint shrugged.

"Satisfaction?"

When they saw the house Ally shook her head again.

"My God, the American dream."

The house was a two-story wood structure with a fence around it. It didn't look large enough to house a man and five wives, not to mention kids.

"This isn't what you want?" he asked.

"The house and the picket fence?" she asked. "Not me."

As they went up the walk, she asked, "Do you suppose all of his wives have had kids?"

"Probably."

"Jesus, a man could have a lot of kids that way."

"Maybe that's what they want."

When Aaron opened the door to their knock he greeted them expansively.

"Ah, my new friends! Come in, come in."

As they entered they immediately became the center of attention. Several women and about six kids stopped to look at them. Clint also saw the man who had first greeted them and directed them to the livery.

"You've met my father-in-law, Daniel," Aaron said.

"Briefly," Clint said, shaking hands with the man.

"I see you found Aaron all right," Daniel said.

"Yes, sir," Clint said. "Your directions were very good."

"And this is Hannah," Aaron said, proudly introducing a handsome woman with dark hair, wearing an apron. "She will be preparing dinner tonight."

"Thank you so much for having us," Ally said to the woman.

"Oh, it's our pleasure," Hannah said.

"Was my son-in-law able to help you with your problem?" Daniel asked.

"We, uh, have some haggling to do," Clint replied.

"Ah, yes, Aaron and his haggling."

"You must come in the kitchen and help," Hannah said to Ally. "The men will go into the living room to do their haggling."

"My grandchildren have possession of the living room," Daniel said.

"I will send Esther out to move them upstairs," Hannah said.

"Come, then," Aaron said, "we'll go into the living room."

The three men entered and another woman, younger, somewhat prettier than the first, came in and shooed away the children, who all seemed to be under ten. Clint found himself wondering how many mothers went with the six children. He also wondered which wife Daniel was the father of.

"I have some nice port," Aaron said. "I can offer you a drink."

"I'll have some if you will."

Aaron looked around and said in a low voice, "Not in the house."

"Then I'll just wait until later," Clint said.

"Have a seat."

The room was cheaply yet comfortably furnished. Clint chose to sit at one end of a sofa that had Daniel at the other end.

"Well, go ahead," Daniel said, "haggle. I'll just observe."

Clint thought that Daniel must be a pretty smart man who knew that his son-in-law needed some contact with the outside world to keep him from becoming too restless. That was why he had immediately commandeered the strangers and sent them to Aaron's livery stable.

A smart man, indeed.

There wasn't much haggling to be done for the wagon wheel. It was really just a formality, but Clint went through the motions and finally got the wheel for what he thought was a good price. After that they all went into the dining room to eat.

Ally served the food, along with Aaron's five wives, and then they all sat and ate. There was no older woman among them, so Clint assumed that Daniel was a widower.

The dinner was very good, and all of the women seemed to be filled with questions for Ally about what was happening in the "outside" world.

"We don't get much in the way of new clothes here," one of them said.

"I got this dress here," Ally replied. "I think it's very nice."

"Probably not as nice as what you are used to," Esther said.

"I think you ladies have badgered our guest enough,"

Aaron said. He looked at Ally. "I apologize. It's not often they get to speak to a young woman from outside."

"You don't get many strangers here?" Clint asked.

"Not many, no," Aaron said.

"But when we do," Esther chimed in, "they usually end up here for dinner."

"We are very curious people, you see," Aaron said. "That's why we ask as many questions as we do."

"Well," Clint said, "we're here to supply what answers we can."

"Well," Aaron said, "I do have one more question for you."

"What is it?"

"Earlier this evening I told a friend of mine, Saul, that you were going to be our guests. Saul is the editor of our local newspaper and he told me something . . . well, that I simply found hard to believe."

"What was that?"

Aaron hesitated, looked around the table, then said, "Well, I'm embarrassed by this, but he told me that you . . . were known for killing people . . . for killing many men. He said they called you . . . what was it?"

"The Gunsmith," Clint said.

"That's right," Aaron said, "that's what he said. But, surely, that is a profession, not a name."

"In my case," Clint said, "it's a little bit of both."

"But . . . I don't understand."

"I am very good with guns," Clint said, "whether it's fixing them or firing them."

"But what of the rumors that you killed many men? Surely that can't be true."

"I've killed my share," Clint said, "but usually they were trying to kill me."

"So . . . this is true then?" Daniel asked. "You are a killer?"

The women at the table suddenly became very agitated, and they rose to begin to clear the table.

"I don't think of myself as a killer," Clint said. "I have killed, but only to save my life, or the life of someone I care about."

"Killing is wrong," Daniel said.

"Well, of course, but—"

"No!" Daniel stood up, throwing his napkin down on the table. "There is no justification for killing!" He glared at Aaron. "You have brought this man to our table, in contact with our family . . . our children!"

Suddenly, he spun and not only left the room but the house, as well. The women, without looking at Clint, hurried into the kitchen.

"This is not fair," Ally said angrily. She stood up. "You're not being fair. Clint is not a bad man. He's not what you—"

She stopped when Clint put his hand on her arm.

"It's all right, Ally," he said. "We should go."

Clint looked across the table at Aaron.

"I'm sorry this happened."

"No," Aaron said, "I am sorry. These people, they are my family, but they are narrow-minded. My father-in-law clings to the old ways—"

"It's all right, really," Clint said. "We'll be leaving in the morning. Can we come by then and pick up the wheel?"

"Of course," Aaron said, also standing. "It is yours. I will not even charge you."

"Oh, no—"

"Please," Aaron said, "it is my way of making up to you the way my family has treated you."

Aaron walked them to the door and saw them out, apologizing again and arranging to meet them at the stable in the morning.

"What horrible people!" Ally said as they walked away.

"Not really."

"They treated you terribly," she said. "How can you be so understanding?"

"They're not used to . . . to what I am, or what I'm supposed to be," Clint said.

"I don't care," she said. Suddenly, something occurred to her. "Do you think Aaron will really meet us in the morning? Do you think they might not give us the wheel we need?"

"I guess we'll find that out in the morning," Clint said, "won't we?"

TWENTY-FIVE

When they returned to their room Ally was still fuming at the treatment Clint had received at the hands of the Mormon family, whose last name they never did learn.

"People like that make me so mad," she said as they entered.

"People like what?" Clint asked, closing the door.

She sat heavily on the bed and looked at her hands, which were in her lap.

"Hypocrites."

"Is that what they are?"

"Well, of course," she said. "They think they're all kind and religious, and then they unfairly judge a man they just met and kick him out of their house. Wouldn't you call that unfair?"

"I suppose I would."

"Then why aren't you angry?"

"Do you get angry when someone calls you a whore?" he asked.

"I guess that depends on their tone of voice," she said, "but I see your point."

"They choose to believe the stories they've heard. I can't fight with them or argue them out of it, and why should I?

Tomorrow morning we'll be leaving here and never coming back.''

''I guess you're right,'' she said. She looked around the room, then back at him. ''There's only one bed.''

''I know,'' he said. ''We can fit, unless you'd rather I slept on the floor.''

''Don't be silly.''

She stood up and started to unbutton her dress.

''You, uh, want me to turn my back? Step outside?''

''Of course I don't want you to step outside,'' she said. ''If you did I'd be all alone in here ... like this.'' She dropped the dress to the floor and was naked. She had a beautiful body, taut and smooth, small but firm breasts, and lovely skin.

''Come to bed, Clint,'' she said. ''I'll make you forget all about those people.''

''Ally—''

''Don't try to argue me out of it,'' she said. ''Tomorrow morning we'll be back with the others and who knows when we'll have another chance like this?''

He wondered if she knew about him and Rachel, but then decided it didn't matter. They were alone in a hotel room, not out in the woods somewhere, sneaking around, and they had the whole night ahead of them.

So why not?

She came to him and began to unbutton his shirt. He didn't stop her. She got it open and eased it off, tossing it aside. She ran her hands over his chest, then kissed it, lingering with her tongue on his nipples.

He unstrapped his holster, reached over, and hung it from the bedpost. She undid his belt, eased his pants down around his ankles, then pushed him into a seated position on the bed. She pulled off his boots and socks, and then the rest of his clothes. By then his penis was stiff and poking up from his pubic hair.

She took it in her hand, stroked it, and said, ''I knew you'd be pretty.''

Her fingertips danced over his smooth, sensitive skin, and then she leaned forward and tenderly kissed the spongy tip. She cradled him in her palm while she kissed the length of him, cupped his balls in her other hand and kissed them as well. Then she worked her way back up the shaft with her tongue, pausing at that tender spot just below the head. After that she wet the tip thoroughly with her saliva, then took him into her mouth, closing her eyes and moaning as he slid down her throat. She took him into her mouth until her nose was nestled against his belly, then withdrew slowly, then took him in again. She did this slowly for a little while, then began to increase the tempo. She could tell when he was ready to explode and released him, giving him one last teasing flick of the tongue.

"Not yet," she said, "I have plans for you. You don't get to finish that fast."

She pushed him down so he was lying on his back and then straddled him. She rubbed her moist slit up and down his penis, wetting him that way, then lifted her hips and came down on him, swallowing him up.

"Ooooh, yes," she said, "it feels so nice. . . ."

It did feel nice. He reached for her, ran his palms over her firm little tits, popped the nipples between his fingers, then thumbed them until they were as hard as pebbles. He sat up then and pulled her to him, so that they were both seated. She arched her back so he could kiss her throat, and work his way down to her nipples, so he could suck and bite them. He felt her tight little bottom on his thighs, which were getting wet from her. He slid his hands beneath her slick buttocks and began to lift her and then let her down, over and over again. Abruptly, she put her hands against his chest and pushed him down onto his back again, then shifted her weight and began to ride him. He squeezed her breasts again as she did so, sliding up and down his hard shaft faster and faster until the sound of flesh slapping flesh filled the room. He suddenly felt like she was sucking his climax from him and as hard as he tried to hold back there was no stopping it. As he exploded inside of her she began to move even faster and then suddenly she caught her breath, stopped just for a moment, eyes wide, and then her own pleasure overtook her and she was once again bouncing on him, this time quite uncontrollably. . . .

TWENTY-SIX

"The others don't have to know about this," she said in the morning.

"I won't tell them," he said, "but they'll probably just have to look at me to know."

"Why?"

"Because you've just about drained the life out of me, Ally. I thought whores didn't like sex because it was their business."

She snuggled closer to him and said, "It's our business when we're with somebody we don't want to be with. Besides, what's not to enjoy? I never had a man do what you did to me last night. Where did you learn to use your mouth and your tongue like that?"

"Practice," he said. "Lots and lots of practice."

"With lots and lots of women, huh?"

"A few."

"And I'll bet they were happy women, too," she said, "like I am."

"I hope so."

"Well, there's been some talk about you among us girls," she said.

"Really?"

"I just wouldn't want them to know yet that I was the

109

first one in your bed. Is that all right with you?"

"That's fine with me, Ally," he said. "The less trouble and tension we have on this trip, the better."

"That's what I think, too."

"Well," he said, "this bed is real warm and cozy, but I think it's time we went and picked up that wheel."

"You really think we're gonna get it?"

"I hope so."

"And he's not gonna charge us?"

"We'll find out."

He started to throw the bedclothes off of them, but she grabbed on to them with one hand and snaked the other hand down between his legs.

"Couldn't we just stay here a little longer?"

"I wish we could," he said, feeling himself respond to her touch, "but if we want that wheel we'd better get going."

She sighed, pouted, and removed her hand. He tossed back the sheets and swung his legs out of bed.

"I'd just like a day or two more with you in a hotel room like this," she said, "or even a better one, in San Francisco."

"Well," he said, pulling on his pants, "we've got a long way to go before we reach San Francisco, so we'd better get moving."

"I'm moving, I'm moving," she said, getting out of bed. She grabbed the same dress she'd been wearing when they got to town, instead of the new one.

"Havin' a new dress will take some explainin' to the others," she said. "Can we put it in your saddlebag for now?"

"Sure thing."

They finished dressing and Ally gave the bed one last, wistful look.

"Most of the men I'm with," she said, "I never want to see another bed when I leave the room. They're fat, or drunk, or both, and they just grunt and groan and squirt, and they think they're real men.''

"Maybe you should try doing something else for a living when you get to San Francisco.''

"Like what?'' she asked. "I have no skills except what I can do in bed.''

"You're smart,'' he said, "you can learn, and I know a lot of people there.''

"You'd help me get a job?''

"Sure,'' he said. "You've got the rest of the trip to think about what you'd like to do. When we get there you tell me, and we'll go from there.''

She kissed his cheek and said, "You really are a nice man, aren't you?''

"I like to think so,'' he said, and they left the room.

TWENTY-SEVEN

When they got to the livery stable Aaron was there, with the wheel. Clint could hear Ally's audible sigh of relief.

"You did not think I would be here," Aaron said. He was speaking to Ally, not Clint.

"Clint did," she said, "I wasn't sure."

"My wife is sorry for what happened."

Ally bit back the words, *Which one?*

"Esther wanted me to give you this." He held out something that was in a wicker basket, covered with a napkin.

"What is it?" Ally asked.

"A peach pie," he said. "She made it for dessert last night—which we never got to eat. She asked me to give it to you."

"Tell her thank you for me," Ally said, puzzled.

Clint had the feeling Esther was going to be very surprised when she realized that pie was missing.

"And now, the wheel. We will tie it to the horse?" Aaron asked.

"Yes," Clint said.

"I'm afraid you'll have to show me . . ." Aaron said, as the two men went into the stable.

Ally lifted the napkin and took a smell. The rest of the girls would be thrilled with this.

•   •   •

When they reached the camp the girls all gathered together anxiously. They cheered when they saw the wheel tied to the third horse.

Under Clint's direction, working together, they were able to lift the wagon so he could slip off the old wheel and put on the new one. Afterwards they made coffee and celebrated with the peach pie.

"And how did you get this wonderful pie?" Gloria asked around a mouthful.

"Someone gave it to us," Ally said.

"They just gave it to you?" Jenny asked, eyeing her slice suspiciously. "What's in it?" She took a sniff.

"Nothing bad," Ally said. "This whole town was made up of Mormons—well, almost the whole town. . . ."

Clint left it to Ally to tell about the town, and the people in it. She even told about being invited to Aaron's home for dinner. What she didn't tell them is what happened after dinner, and what happened between them in the hotel room.

Later, Gloria came over and sat next to him while Ally continued to field questions about Mormons.

"Why do I get the feeling there's more to this story?" she asked.

"There is," he said, "but it's got nothing to do with the wheel. Do you want to hear it?"

Gloria hesitated, then said, "I don't think so. Should we get moving today?"

"Yes," he said. "There's still plenty of daylight ahead of us."

"You did buy that wheel, right?" she asked. "Nobody's going to be coming after it?"

"You mean, did I steal it, like you stole the wagon?" he asked.

"You're right," she said, "it wasn't a fair question. Sorry."

"Gloria," he said, "nobody's going to be coming after the wheel, don't worry."

"Ally looks . . . different."

"I wonder why that is?"

Clint looked over at where the women were sitting, still pumping Ally for information. They all seemed excited except for Rachel. She kept looking from Clint to Ally and back again, as if she was trying to figure something out.

Clint hoped she never did.

TWENTY-EIGHT

They left the broken wheel by the trail and continued on westward. Clint rode alongside the wagon for a while to observe the new wheel, and when he was satisfied that it would hold he rode on ahead. If he'd been scouting ahead before the wheel got broken he might have been able to pick an easier route. He'd learned his lesson and didn't want any more forced stops along the way.

But, of course, he knew that was just when forced stops happened.

They camped that night, and Kathy cooked up some bacon and beans. During dinner the women were lamenting that they didn't have any more peach pie for afterward.

"You can have all the peach pie, apple pie, or blueberry pie you want when you reach San Francisco," Clint told them.

"I don't see how men can stay on the trail so long and eat this way," Rachel said.

"Some men aren't used to anything better," he said.

"Well," she said, "if we had a proper kitchen I could show you something better."

"Rachel's a wonderful cook," Miriam said.

"Is that a fact?" Clint asked. It was something Rachel

117

had not mentioned to him. "Good enough to do it for a living?"

"Better," Rachel said, "but cooking for other people isn't something I ever wanted to do."

She looked around then and spoke before anyone else could.

"Okay, okay, being a whore isn't something I thought I'd want to do, either."

"What about being a cook in San Francisco?" Clint asked.

"Oh, sure, and who would hire a whore to be a cook?" she asked.

"Well, first of all there'd be no reason to tell them you were a whore."

"You mean lie?" Rachel asked.

"You've never lied to a man before?" Jenny asked.

"Not about what I was," Rachel said. "I've been a whore for a long time, and while I may not like it, I ain't ashamed of it."

"Ain't proud of it, either," Kathy said. "Leastways, I ain't. If I could get another kind of job in San Francisco I'd do it."

"Clint knows people in San Francisco," Ally said. "He said he could help get me a job there. I'll bet he could help all of us."

"You know that many people, Clint?" Gloria asked.

"I know people who run hotels and saloons and casinos," he said. "I'll bet any of you girls could work in any of those places."

"In a hotel," Jenny said. "Doin' what? Changing the sheets on the bed? I'd rather be a whore."

"Not me," Miriam said. "I'd rather change sheets."

"That's 'cause you didn't grow up doin' that, little girl," Jenny said.

"Don't yell at her just because you grew up changing other people's beds, Jenny," Rachel said.

"She wasn't yelling at me," Miriam said, "were you, Jenny?"

Jenny hesitated, then smiled at Miriam and said, "No, baby girl, I sure wasn't."

"Why don't we get some sleep and talk about this tomorrow?" Gloria suggested.

"I'll take a watch tonight, Gloria," Clint said. "After all, I got to spend last night in a real bed."

"So did I," Ally said quickly, and then realized how that might have sounded. "I mean . . . uh, I can take a watch, too."

"Fine," Gloria said, "and I'll take one. The rest of you girls can sleep all night."

"Praise God," Jenny said.

As they were moving into their sleeping positions for the night, Rachel passed real close to Clint and asked in a low voice, "Separate beds?"

When Clint turned she was gone.

Gloria came over to him and asked, "Do you want the first watch?"

"Sure, I'll take it," Clint said.

"Did you mean what you told Ally? About getting her a job, I mean."

"Yes, I meant it," he said. "I meant it for all of you—that is, any of you that want to change professions."

"I'm sure some of us will take you up on that, Clint," she said. "You'd better start thinking about which friends you're going to put the touch on."

He did think about that while he was on watch. He also wondered which of the girls would want to change jobs and which ones wouldn't.

TWENTY-NINE

"I thought you said they was gonna be easy to follow, Caleb," Ab Nevers complained.

"I thought they would be."

Nevers looked down at the broken wheel and kicked at it.

"Why are we still about three days behind them, then?" he asked.

Caleb and Nevers had ridden ahead of the rest to do some scouting. That was when they found the cold camp and the broken wheel.

"They broke a wheel," Nevers said, "and had to replace it. That must've taken a day. Why are we still three behind?"

"What are you saying, Ab?" Caleb demanded. "You sayin' I ain't doin' my job?"

"Caleb," Nevers said, facing the bigger, older man squarely, "I'm rememberin' that you were kind of sweet on one of those whores. Which one was it? Kathy, wasn't it? Huh?"

"So?"

"So maybe you ain't tryin' so hard to find them," Nevers said. "Maybe you want them to get away from Carthage."

Nevers could tell from the look in Caleb's eyes that he'd hit the nail right on the head.

"You do, don't you?"

"She didn't belong there, Ab," Caleb said. "She . . . she never did."

"She's a whore, Caleb," Nevers said. "Where else would she belong?"

"Someplace fine," Caleb said.

Caleb Manson was in his forties and by any standards was an ugly man. The whore Kathy, however, had never treated him like he was ugly, and he had never mistreated her—not the way the rest of Swallow's men did. They seemed to feel that those women were not only there to fuck, but to knock around, as well. Caleb started seeing Kathy regularly to keep that from happening to her at the hands of the others.

And it was true, he was sweet on her.

"Caleb," Nevers said. "Look. I ain't gonna say anything to Ben about this, but you got to start doin' your job from here on out, you hear?"

"I hear, Ab."

"Ben ever found out about this, he'd skin you," Nevers said.

"I appreciate you not tellin' him."

"I ain't gonna say a word," Nevers said, "long as we start closing ground on them whores. Okay?"

"Okay, Ab."

Nevers turned at the sound of horses and saw Ben Swallow and the others riding down on them.

"What are you gonna tell 'im?" Caleb asked.

"I'll think of somethin'," Nevers said. "Don't you worry about it."

"So it's like we thought?" Swallow asked later.

"Yep," Nevers said. "I knew he was sweet on one of them whores."

"Did you straighten him out?"

"I did," Nevers said. "I think we'll start makin' better time now. I told him you'd skin him if you found out."

"And I will," Swallow said, "when this is all over."

Swallow looked over to where the other men were, gathered around the broken wheel.

"They probably had to go into Gentry to get that wheel. What do we know about that town?"

"Lots of Mormons."

Swallow rubbed his hand over his gray/black stubble.

"I want you to go into town and see what you can find out. Take one of the others with you."

"What is it you think I'll find out, Ben?"

"Maybe where they've headed," Swallow said. "If we knew that, we could get there first and be waitin' for them."

"Why would they tell somebody that?"

"I don't know, Ab," Swallow said. "Why don't you go into town like I told you and find out."

"Okay."

"We'll keep ridin' and camp in a while. You'll be able to catch up."

"All right, Ben," Nevers said. "What are you gonna do about Caleb?"

"Nothin' . . . yet."

THIRTY

Clint was starting to find it uncomfortable to be around Rachel and Ally. He constantly found them looking at him, and kept wondering which of the other girls they had told about what happened. After all, women talked about those things with each other, didn't they? Did Ally have a best friend out of the other girls? Did Rachel? Not that he had noticed. The only thing he did notice was that they were all pretty protective about Miriam. He even wondered at one point if they all might have taken off from Carthage just to get Miriam away from there.

On the third night since leaving Gentry with their new wheel Clint had the first watch, and he had to wake Ally for the second.

"I hope you're not mad at me," she said.

"Why would I be?"

"You seem to be avoiding me."

They were whispering so as not to wake the others.

"I'm not avoiding you."

"Well, I thought you might be upset because I told the others about the job you were going to get me."

"That's just silly," he said. "I'll be happy to get jobs for as many of you as wants them."

"We'll all appreciate it, Clint."

"Ally, I have to ask you . . . did you tell anyone about what happened between us in Gentry?"

"No," she said, her eyes widening.

"Not even one girl? Your best friend?"

"I don't have a best friend," she said, "but I see what you're getting at. You think girls confide these things to each other all the time."

"Well, don't they?"

"No," she said, "well, sometimes, but not all the time."

"And which is this?"

"What?"

"Sometime or all the time?"

She frowned a moment, then said, "Oh, I see . . . no, no I swear, I haven't told a soul."

"Okay, good," he said. "I'm going to turn in."

"You know," she said, giving him a sly look, "they're all pretty sound sleepers. We could slip away and—"

"Shame on you," he said, cutting her off. "If you were in the army you could be shot for such a thing."

"Well," she said, "I guess it's a good thing I'm not in the army—but you can't shoot me for thinkin' something, can you?"

"No," Clint said. "Good night, Ally."

He rolled himself into his bedroll so she couldn't see the telltale sign that he was thinking about that night in the hotel, too.

THIRTY-ONE

Ab Nevers and Zack Wilson rode into Gentry together while Swallow and the rest traveled on.

"What are we supposed to find out here?" Wilson asked again.

"If anyone knows where Adams and the whores are headed," Nevers said.

"Who do we ask?"

"Well, they came in to buy a wheel," Nevers said. "Let's go to the livery."

They found the livery and a man came out to greet them.

"That one of them Mormons?" Wilson asked.

"Looks like it."

"Can I help you?" Aaron asked. "Do you need a place for your horses for the night?"

"We ain't stayin'," Wilson said.

"We're lookin' for a friend of ours," Nevers said.

"And who would that be?"

"His name's Clint Adams," Nevers said.

"He's riding with six whores," Wilson said, before Nevers could stop him.

"With six . . ."

"Women," Nevers said. "Six women, my friend meant to say."

127

"That is a harsh thing to say about women," Aaron said, scolding Zack Wilson for what he thought was an opinion on the man's part.

"Have you seen him?"

"Why, yes," Aaron said, "but your friend was not here with six women, just one, and she was his wife. So you must be mistaken."

"You know," Nevers said, "I guess we are, friend. By the way, does this town have a lawman?"

"We are all law-abiding citizens," Aaron said. "We have no need of an official law keeper."

"I see. Interesting. Tell me, how long did Clint and the woman stay?" Nevers thought this was going to be too easy.

"Just overnight. They stayed at the hotel, but had dinner at my house."

"Really? Did they talk much?"

"Some," Aaron said. "Clint spoke with me and my father-in-law, and Ally went into the kitchen with my wives."

"Wives?" Zack Wilson repeated.

"Yes," Aaron said, "I have five."

"Five wives?"

Aaron laughed.

"We are aware that some people find our ways . . . odd," he said.

"Odd ain't the word, mister," Wilson said.

"Could we talk with your wives?" Nevers asked. "We'd really like to find out where Clint and his . . . wife were heading."

"If you're his friends," Aaron said, "shouldn't you know where he's going?"

"Well, we don't," Wilson said. "Maybe one of your wives does."

"Gentlemen," Aaron said, "I hope you don't take offense at this, but I really don't think I want you talking to my wives."

"You know what, pilgrim?" Wilson said, drawing his gun and pointing it at Aaron. "I do take offense at that—real bad!"

The door to Aaron's home sprang open from a kick and Aaron went sprawling onto the floor from a push from Zack Wilson. Wilson and Nevers stepped in after him.

Daniel, Esther, Hannah, and the other wives—not to mention the children—all froze.

"These your wives?" Wilson asked. In an exaggerated gesture he removed his hat and said, "Ladies. A pleasure."

"What have you done to my husband?" Esther demanded.

Aaron was still lying on the floor, blood oozing from a cut on his forehead, compliments of Zack Wilson's gun sight.

"Get out of this house—" Daniel said, starting toward the two armed men.

"That wouldn't be a smart thing to do, old man," Ab Nevers said. "Not unless you want somebody to get hurt."

"Momma," one of the little boys said, "make them go away."

"Hello, little boy," Zack said. "Which one of these ladies is your momma? Or are they all your momma?"

The little boy's eyes grew wide, and he shrank back against Hannah's leg.

"I guess you're his momma," Wilson said, eyeing her appreciatively. He thought she was the prettiest of the five wives.

"W-what do you want?" Esther demanded, stepping between Wilson and Hannah.

"Ladies," Ab Nevers said, "we're not here to cause any trouble. We just need some information."

"What kind of information?" Daniel asked.

"The kind you don't have, old man," Zack Wilson said, "so shut up. We're talkin' to the ladies."

"We're looking for Clint Adams," Nevers said. "Your

husband said he was here and that his woman was in the kitchen with you."

"I told you that man would bring us trouble!" Daniel blurted at his semiconscious son-in-law.

"All we need to know," Nevers said, "is if his woman said anything about where they were going when they left here."

Nobody answered.

"Somebody's got to have an answer," Nevers said, "or my friend here is going to have to take each of you ladies into the other room and ask you personally."

"Startin' with you, pretty lady," Wilson said, leering at Hannah.

"There won't be any need for that," Esther said.

"Oh?" Nevers asked. "And why not?"

"I know where they were going."

"Well, that's good, ma'am," Nevers said. "That's real good. All you got to do is tell me where, and me and my friend will be on our way."

"Esther," Daniel said, "tell him—quickly!"

Esther hesitated and looked down at Aaron, wishing he were conscious so he could tell her if she was doing the right thing.

THIRTY-TWO

Clint woke that morning to the smell of coffee. Rachel was up first and had put the pot on, and he had to admit that her coffee was the best out of everyone's, including his own. Of course, trail coffee was usually as black as it gets, and thick, but not always tasty. Rachel managed to avoid that last part.

"Here you go," she said, as he approached the fire.

"Thanks."

"You were with her, weren't you?"

"What?"

"In Gentry," Rachel said. "You were with Ally, in the same hotel room, in the same bed. It had to happen."

"Rachel."

"I was first, though," she said. "Remember that!"

She hissed that last part at him because others were approaching, and then she turned with a smile to pour everyone coffee and inquire if they wanted flapjacks for breakfast. She was also the only one who offered a variety. The others always made bacon for breakfast and beans for dinner.

Clint wondered why it was so important to her to be acknowledged as the first one he'd slept with. He decided that sleeping with her had been a mistake, and the night

131

with Ally had compounded it. That was it, he wasn't going to be with any of the others.

Although the one he'd had his eye on since meeting them all had been Gloria, and she showed absolutely no interest in being with him. He admired not only her beauty, but her strength, as well. Maybe in San Francisco . . .

He wondered if Jenny, Kathy, and Miriam thought about being with him. Well, Miriam probably did. After all she still had a huge crush on him. As for Jenny, she didn't seem to like white men. As for Kathy, she'd given him no indication so far that she was interested.

He decided this was silly. After all, he was not traveling with his own private harem. It was silly to think he had a chance to bed all these women before they got to San Francisco.

What kind of a fiasco would that be when they all found out?

He was starting to be sorry that he'd given them all shooting lessons.

THIRTY-THREE

When Ben Swallow awoke that morning he looked around and saw Zack Wilson in his bedroll, sleeping soundly.

"Where's Ab?" he bellowed, rolling out.

"Here!" Nevers shouted. He was hunkered down by the fire, coffeepot in hand.

"Pour me a cup of that," Swallow said, staggering over. He was getting too damned old to be sleeping on the ground and drinking trail coffee, but it was the only thing that got him started in the morning.

"You boys got in pretty late last night," he said, accepting the cup from Nevers.

"Yeah."

"Did you find out what we wanted?"

"We did."

"Why'd it take you so long?"

"Ben," Nevers said. "Zack got a little carried away yesterday."

"Oh? How?"

"Well, this town was mostly Mormons, and this one fella had five wives, and one of them knew where Adams and the whore went, but another was real pretty and Zack kinda took a shine to her—"

"Don't tell me."

133

"Yeah," Nevers said. "I'm afraid so."

"You couldn't stop him?"

"We couldn't afford to fight each other in front of them," Nevers said.

"So he raped one of them?"

Nevers rubbed his nose.

"Ab?"

"He didn't stop at one," Nevers said. "He's a bit of a bull, you know, when he gets . . . like that."

"How many?"

"Two." Zack had taken Hannah into one of the bedrooms, and when he came out suddenly one of the other wives looked good to him, too. In the end not only Aaron but Daniel had ended up on the floor, bleeding from a head wound.

"Did he kill either of them?"

"No."

"Well, that's good, anyway. Anyone see it?"

"Well, yeah," Nevers said. "I mean, not the actual rape, but there were two men, five women, and about six kids."

"Kids?"

"Little ones."

"Girls?"

"A couple."

"Did he touch them?"

"Hell, no!" Nevers spat. "I wouldn'ta stood for that, Ben."

"What about law?"

"No law in the town."

"None at all?"

"Nope."

"Appears to me you boys lucked out."

"I guess."

"Why don't they have any law?"

"They say they're all law-abidin' citizens," Nevers said. "Ben, there wasn't a gun in the house."

Swallow sipped his coffee, deep in thought for a moment.

"So ain't no law gonna be comin' after you?" he asked.

"Unless they go to a marshal or somebody, I don't see it."

Swallow dumped the remnants of his coffee into the fire, causing it to flare.

"Okay," he said, "where are they headed?"

"San Francisco."

"How do we know that?"

"Adams took one of the women to town with him, passed her off as his wife. They got invited to dinner, and she told some of the wives they were going to San Francisco to start a new life."

"You believe this woman when she told you this?"

"I did," Nevers said. "She was scared."

"And this was before Zack raped anybody?"

"That's right."

"Okay, then," Swallow said, "wake the others and let's get movin'."

"We goin' to San Francisco?"

"I ain't decided yet," Swallow said. "It's a big place, lots of law. We should be able to catch up with them before they get there, now that you talked with Caleb and we know where they're goin'."

Nevers stood up, preparing to wake the others.

"You gonna say anything to Zack?"

Swallow reached for the pot. He wanted to get another cup before the others got to it.

"I'm gonna wait and see if he says anything to me," he said.

"Damn fool's pecker might end up gettin' us in trouble someday," Never said.

"I'll see to it, Ab," Swallow said. "I'll see to Zack and to Caleb, when this is all over."

"Okay, Ben," Nevers said. "It's still your show."

"Don't forget it, boy," Swallow said. "It's always gonna be my show."

THIRTY-FOUR

"What's wrong?" Gloria asked Clint.

He was riding Duke right alongside the wagon while she was driving, and she must have noticed the look on his face. She was astute that way.

"I don't know," he said. "I just got a bad feeling." Things had been going too well for the past two days. Maybe that's what was grating on him.

"About what?"

"About someone coming up behind us," he said.

She craned her neck to look behind them.

"You can't see anyone," he said. "I just . . . feel them."

"Has this happened with you before?"

"Oh, yeah."

"And are you usually right?"

"Usually," he said. "My instincts have kept me alive this long."

"What should we do, then?"

"I'll take a ride back and see what I can see," he said. "You just keep going."

She reached out and grabbed his arm.

"What if you don't come back?"

He thought he saw real fear in her eyes for the first time.

Maybe it had always been there, and she just wasn't hiding it as well at that moment.

"I'll be back," he said. "I'm just going to take a look a few miles behind us to see if I'm right."

"And if you are?"

"We'll think of something."

Clint rode back a few hours. It was all he needed. The ground was flat, and he was able to see the clouds of dust the riders were kicking up, even though they were hours away. They were probably a half a day behind the wagon, and there were more of them than he liked to think about.

He looked down at the ground and saw the tracks their wagon was leaving. Tracks a blind man could have followed—and Ben Swallow was no blind man.

"Shit," he said, and wheeled Duke around. He was going to have to get into the big gelding just to be able to get back to the wagon in time to figure out something before Swallow and his men caught up.

When he got back to the wagon he told the women what he'd seen.

"How long do we have?" Gloria asked.

"At this pace, maybe half a day—maybe less. Six, eight hours, even."

"What if we increase our pace?"

"We can't outrun them," Clint said. "That might buy us an hour or two more, but we might kill the horses."

"How many men are there?" Rachel asked. They kept the wagon moving. The other women had crowded to the front of the wagon to hear the news.

"Couldn't tell, but a cloud of dust like that, could be six, maybe more."

"Can you handle six men?" Miriam asked.

"What a dumb question," Jenny said. "Course he can't. Nobody can."

"I didn't think he could handle three," Kathy said, "and

he did. I don't think it was such a dumb question.''

"Well, the answer's no," Clint said, "not unless half of them are blind and the other half are crippled.''

"So what are we supposed to do?" Gloria asked.

"We've got guns," Jenny said. "We can make a stand.''

"We only have one rifle," Clint said. "They each have a rifle. They could stay out of reach of the handguns and just pick us off.''

"I don't think they want us dead," Gloria said.

"That wouldn't apply to me, though," Clint said.

"Then why don't you just go?" Gloria suggested. "You can get away. There's no point in you getting killed for us.''

"Leaving you is not an option," he said, "so forget it.''

"Then what is an option?" Gloria asked.

"And how many do we have?" Jenny asked.

"Not many," Clint said, "not that many at all.''

"Then what are we going to do?" Miriam asked, and her fear was naked for all to see. "I don't want to go back, Clint.''

Clint considered cutting the team loose, having the girls ride double, and one with him, but that still left one extra.

"What are you thinking?" Gloria asked.

"That the six of you could ride these three horses," he said.

"And what about you?"

"I could hold them off.''

"For how long?" Gloria asked. "We're a long way from San Francisco, Clint. You couldn't hold them off until we got there.''

"I know," he said, "I know. I'm just thinking out loud here. We should have gotten rid of this wagon long ago. This is my fault.''

"Never mind whose fault it is," Gloria said. "This is not the time for that.''

"What if they do kill us?" Miriam asked. "I don't want to die.''

"We're not going to die," Gloria said. *Not all of us, anyway,* she thought. If they took them back to Carthage, she knew that he would kill her. Maybe not the others, but definitely her.

"I've got an idea," she said.

"Let's hear it."

"You said six people could ride double."

"That still leaves one extra," he said. "I thought of that—"

"He wants me."

"What?"

"Ted really wants me," she said. "If they catch me, maybe they'll let the rest of you go."

Suddenly the girls were all shouting at one time. The word Clint heard most of all was, "No!"

"Listen to me!" Gloria said. "I'm the one he feels betrayed by. Don't you see?"

"What we see," Jenny said, "is that we're all going forward together or back together." She looked at Clint. "I think Gloria is right. You should ride on and leave us. They'll just take us back."

"If you leave me and the wagon, you can get away," Gloria said.

"We're not doing that," Jenny said.

"We can't!" Miriam said.

"Forget it!" Rachel said.

Suddenly, Gloria reined in the team.

"What are you doing?" Clint asked.

"I have something to tell you," she said, "all of you, and when I'm finished you might *want* to leave me behind."

They all stared at her expectantly.

THIRTY-FIVE

"How much?" Clint asked.

Gloria hesitated, then said, "Sixty-eight thousand."

"Dollars?!" Jenny asked.

Gloria nodded.

"Where is it?" Rachel asked.

"It's in the wagon," Gloria said. "Under the floor-boards."

"Can we see it?" Rachel asked.

"I've never seen that much money," Miriam said.

"Now's not the time," Clint said. "Besides, aren't you mad at her?"

"Why should we be mad?" Miriam asked.

"She put all of your lives in jeopardy—and mine—by not telling us about it sooner. Besides, she *stole* sixty-eight thousand dollars and didn't tell any of you."

"She did it for us," Miriam said.

"So we'd have some money to start fresh," Ally said.

"How do you know that?" Clint asked. "How do you know she didn't take it for herself, and wasn't going to share it with any of you?"

Miriam shook her head and said simply, "Gloria wouldn't do that."

And they all seemed to agree, even Jenny.

He looked at Gloria, who gave him a wan smile.

"I knew we'd need money when we got settled," she said, "and I knew where he kept this money. It was like an emergency fund for him."

"Okay," Clint said, "tell me this. Do you think Swallow and his boys know about the money?"

"Oh, no," Gloria said, "Ted would never tell them. They'd keep it for sure."

Clint wasn't sure what to suggest now so he said, "Let's keep moving."

They started forward again.

"This doesn't solve our problem," Jenny said.

"Yes, it does," Gloria said. "If I let them take me back—"

"How are you going to let them take you and the money back," Clint asked, "without telling them about the money? They'd kill you as soon as they saw it."

Gloria thought for a moment, then said, "Oh."

"Oh is right," Clint said. "Forget about staying behind."

"What if we give the money back?" Miriam asked.

"What?" Gloria said.

"We just said we can't let Ben Swallow and his men find out about it—" Rachel started.

"No," Miriam said, "I mean, what if we contacted Mr. Carthage and told him we'd send the money back? Banks can send money to other banks, can't they?"

"Yes, they can," Clint said.

"Give it back?" Jenny asked.

"All of it?" Rachel asked.

"All or none," Clint said. "It's got to be one way or the other." He looked at Gloria. "Would he accept?"

"I don't think so," she said.

"Why not?"

"Because it's more than the money," she answered. "I think he wants me almost as much as the money."

"And us?" Jenny asked.

"Sure, he'd like to have all of us back," Gloria said, "but in order of importance I'd say it's me, the money, and the rest of you."

"Maybe," Clint said, "you're putting too much importance on yourself, Gloria. I think this is worth a try."

"How do we do it, then?" Jenny asked.

"First we have to find the nearest town," he said. "Then we have to hope it has three things."

"What three things?" Rachel asked.

"A bank, a telegraph line . . . and some law."

"Why law?" Jenny asked.

"Because," Clint explained, "we're going to need the law to keep Swallow and his boys off of us while we contact Carthage."

"But do we have time to make it to a town?" Jenny asked.

"I don't know," Clint said. "I guess we're just going to have to keep going and find out. I saw a road sign further back. In about another hour we'll be in Nevada. I know Nevada pretty well."

"And we have an hour to spare," Gloria said, "don't we?"

"We have several," Clint said.

"So then," Jenny said, "it's a race to a big enough town. If we make it we've got a chance."

"And if they catch up to us first," Rachel said, "we don't."

"That's the way it shapes up, ladies," Clint said. He looked behind them but couldn't see a cloud of dust yet. "Let's keep our fingers crossed."

THIRTY-SIX

They crossed into Nevada two hours later. By that time Clint was able to make out the cloud of dust behind them.

"They're closing in faster than I thought," he said.

"Could they see us from there?" Gloria asked.

"No," he said, "and we're not moving fast enough to kick up a noticeable cloud of dust, but they've got our tracks to follow."

"Will they be able to tell how far ahead of them we are by the tracks?" she asked.

"Oh, yeah," he said, "a good tracker will know how old they are."

"What if we split up?" she asked. "You go one way and we take the wagon another way."

"They'd follow the wagon."

"You'd be safe."

"Don't start that again," he said. "Let's just keep moving. We should come to a town soon."

"Ben, can I ask you a question?" Ab Nevers said.

"Go ahead."

"You think Carthage is having us go through this just for a half a dozen whores? Or a stolen wagon?"

"No," Swallow said, "I don't."

145

"What do you figure it is?"

Swallow looked behind them, to see if the other men were within earshot. Caleb Manson was riding ahead of them, out of sight.

"I figure these whores took somethin' of his," Swallow said. "Somethin' he wants back pretty bad."

"Like what, for instance? Money, do you think?"

"I think," Swallow said.

"It must be a lot."

"That's what I'm thinkin'," Swallow said. "You're gettin' pretty smart, boy."

"So what do you think we should do when we catch up to that wagon?"

"I think we should tear it apart and see what we find," Swallow said.

"And if we find money? And a lot of it?"

Swallow looked at Nevers.

"I guess we'll cross that road when we come to it, boy. Meanwhile, let's just keep this little conversation between you and me, shall we?"

"Fine by me."

About a half hour later Caleb Manson came riding back to Swallow and the rest.

"We got 'em!" he said excitedly.

"How far ahead?" Swallow asked.

"Maybe two hours."

"That means they can see our dust," Swallow said. "Ab, have the men spread out. Let's keep from makin' one big cloud and see if that confuses them."

"Right, Ben."

"Want me to stay on their trail, Ben?" Caleb asked.

"Yeah, Caleb," Swallow said, giving the man a cold stare, "you do that."

For just a moment Caleb wondered if Swallow knew what he had done . . . but Ab had said he wasn't going to tell. It must've been his imagination.

• • •

"What's wrong?" Gloria asked Clint.

"I don't see the dust cloud anymore."

He was peering behind them intently, a worried look on his face.

"Could they have given up?" Jenny asked hopefully.

"No," he said, "it's more likely they spread out, so they wouldn't make one big cloud."

"What's that mean?" Gloria asked.

"It means they know they're close," Clint said. "They're trying to spook us."

"What makes them think we even noticed a cloud of dust?" Gloria asked.

"They know I'm with you," Clint said. "They know I'd notice."

"What do we do?"

Clint looked at her worried face.

"All we can do is keep moving, Gloria," he said.

"And pray," Miriam added.

"That doesn't sound like such a bad idea."

Within a half hour Clint thought that Miriam's prayers had been answered. They came to a road sign that said: TUCK-ERSVILLE, 10 MILES. Beneath that it said: POP. 2,000.

"That's a big place," Gloria said.

"Big enough for our purposes," Clint said. "Ladies, I think we bought ourselves a little bit of a reprieve."

THIRTY-SEVEN

When they pulled into Tuckersville, Nevada, the team pulling the wagon was blowing hard and Gloria's arms were trembling with tension. They didn't attract that much attention because most of the women were inside the wagon. All anybody saw was two women on a wagon and a man on a big black gelding.

They found the livery and pulled to a stop in front of it. The liveryman came out of the stable just in time to see Clint help each girl down from the wagon in turn. By the time the sixth girl's feet hit the ground the man's eyes had bugged out.

"Do you have someplace we can leave our wagon?" Clint asked him.

"Uh, sure, out back."

"And will you take care of the horses?"

"Sure."

"Be careful with mine," Clint said. "He'll take off a finger."

The man held up one of his hands and showed Clint that he had four and a half fingers on it, as well as some other scars from sharp teeth.

"Been done before," he said.

"Thanks. Can we settle up afterwards?"

"Why not?" the man asked. He was about sixty, with a fringe of white hair and oddly red ears. "You mind if I ask you—"

"They're my daughters," Clint said.

"All of 'em?" the man asked.

"Except me," Gloria said. "I'm the stepmother."

"Pleasure to meet you, ma'am."

Clint removed his rifle and saddlebags from his saddle before the liveryman led Duke into the stable.

"While he's inside," he said to the women, "get those guns I bought you and keep them in the folds of your skirts."

Gloria and Jenny were the ones who did that.

"What about the money?" Rachel whispered.

"It's been safe in the wagon up to now," Clint said. "We'll just leave it there."

"What do we do now?" Kathy asked.

"Well, first we have to find a hotel with four rooms available," Clint said. "After that we'll have to do some talking to figure out our next move. I'm leaning toward talking to the local law."

"But we can't—" Jenny started, but Clint cut her off.

"Let's wait until we're inside to argue about it. Come on."

They found a hotel that had rooms available and Clint booked four of them. One for him, and one each for two of the women. Gloria and Miriam took one, Kathy and Ally the second, and Jenny and Rachel the third. When they were checked in they all gathered in one room, Clint's.

"Can't we do this in the dining room?" Rachel asked. "I'd like to get some real food."

"One man and six women attracts attention," Clint said. "Look at how people were looking at us on the street. When we're done here the six of you can go and get something to eat."

"And take baths," Jenny said. "I feel like I've got dirt comin' out my—well, there's a lot of dirt."

"And what are you gonna do?" Gloria asked.

"Well," he replied, "like I said before, I'm thinking about going to the law."

"But the money—" Jenny started.

"Gloria, did Carthage come by that money legally?"

"I doubt it."

"Then I doubt he's told the law about it," Clint said. "Besides, I don't think he's going to want anyone to know that—and you'll excuse me, ladies—a bunch of whores took off with his money."

"So what will you tell the local sheriff?" Gloria asked.

"I guess I'll have to figure that out," he said. "Trust me?"

"At this point?" Gloria asked, then looked at the other girls and received a message from them. "Why not?"

THIRTY-EIGHT

Clint left the hotel and walked over to the sheriff's office. He expected to have a plan by the time he got there. He didn't. He was just going to have to improvise.

He entered and found himself inside a sheriff's office unlike any he'd ever seen before. It was the same size as most of them, but the furnishings were unusual. In fact, they looked like they had come out of a whorehouse. There was a red sofa against one wall, and the desk looked like expensive cherry wood. In front of the desk was a Queen Anne chair, also red with what looked like gold studs all along it.

"I know," the man behind the desk said, "it looks like a whorehouse."

Clint looked at the man. At least he looked normal, a dark-haired man in his thirties with a tin star pinned to a brown leather vest worn over a blue shirt.

"I'm Sheriff Randy Taylor," he said. "What can I do for you, aside from explaining these furnishings?"

"Is it a long explanation?"

"No," Taylor said. "My predecessor closed down the local whorehouse and confiscated their furnishings. You should see the silk sheets in the cells."

"Are you kidding?"

"Go take a look."

Clint shook his head.

"I'll take your word for it. Sheriff, my name's Clint Adams."

"Adams," Taylor said, sitting up straighter. "The Gunsmith?"

"That's right."

"What brings you to Tuckersville, Mr. Adams? Not looking for trouble, I hope."

"I'm not looking for it," Clint said, "but I'm afraid it's on my tail."

"And you've come to me for help?"

"If you can give me some."

Taylor sat back and regarded Clint curiously.

"I've got to hear why the Gunsmith needs my help. Have a seat and start talking."

Clint looked at the red Queen Anne chair, then sat in it and started talking. Even at that point he didn't know what was going to come out of his mouth. . . .

"So let me get this straight," Taylor said when Clint was finished with his story. "You're escorting these women to San Francisco?"

"That's right."

"And they're whores."

"Prostitutes."

"Okay, prostitutes. And their former employer has sent Ben Swallow and his men to bring them back?"

"That's right."

"Why would Swallow be interested?"

"Well, from what I understand, he and his men used this whorehouse quite frequently."

"And the girls worked for . . . who?"

"A man named Carthage."

"That's right," Taylor said, "and he has a whole county named after him and . . . how many towns?"

"Five."   •

"Five," Taylor said, nodding.

To Clint's utter surprise he had told Sheriff Taylor the truth, leaving out only the part about the money.

"Are you aware that this sounds crazy?"

"Oh, yes," Clint said, "very aware. But Swallow and his men are due here very soon, and I think that will be all the proof you need."

"Well, I guess there's only one thing I can say to all of this," Taylor said.

"And what's that?"

The sheriff stood up and said, "Get those women out of my town . . . pronto!"

THIRTY-NINE

"What?"

"You heard me," Taylor said. "I won't have Ben Swallow and his men shooting up this town because of a bunch of whores."

"Sheriff," Clint said, "maybe you don't understand. I've got six women who need help—"

"Then you help 'em," Taylor said. "That's what you signed on for. Why do you think these furnishings are in this office? This town won't have anything to do with whores, Adams. We haven't had a whorehouse here in five years."

"These women are not looking to set up business here, Sheriff," Clint said. "They just need some rest and some protection—"

"Again," Taylor said, "protection is your department."

"Don't you have some deputies?"

"I have two, and one is as green as they come."

"And the other?"

"He won't have anything to do with this, and neither will I. We'd both lose our jobs."

"I can't believe this," Clint said. "It's your job to protect people—"

"It's my job to protect the people of this town, Adams,"

Taylor said, "not every wagonload of whores that comes rolling in."

Clint stared at the lawman for a few moments, long enough for the man to decide to sit down and find something of interest on his desk.

"All right, Sheriff," Clint said, "you've made yourself very clear."

"Good."

"Now let me make myself clear," he went on. "I don't have time to get those women back into the wagon and out of your town even if I wanted to. So what I intend to do is make a stand here. That means me against six men, maybe more."

"They'll kill you."

"Maybe," Clint said, "but I'll kill some of them. In the meantime, the town *will* get shot up, and maybe some of your citizens will get killed."

"Goddamn it—"

"You have time to get hold of your deputies and post them on the street. Maybe even swear in a couple more. When Swallow rides in if he sees a show of force from the law he'll think twice before acting. That's all I need. I don't need you to arrest him, I don't need you and your men to face him, I only need for you to give him pause long enough for me to talk to him."

Taylor worried the inside of his cheek so hard Clint thought he'd chew through it.

"That's all?"

"That's it. Nobody even needs to know about the women. All the people of this town will know is that a force of men rode in, and you put your men on the streets as a precaution."

"You don't think Swallow will throw down on my men?"

"I don't think he wants to tangle with the law," Clint said. "He and his men walk a thin line, and they're not going to want to cross over it if they don't have to. It would interfere with future business.''

Taylor switched to the other side of his cheek.

''If you're going to do it, you'd better get moving,'' Clint said. ''They'll be here anytime. If you're not going to do it, you'd better get ready to do some repairs on your town when it's all over.''

''Damn it, damn it,'' Taylor said, standing up. ''I'll get my men on the street.''

''Give them rifles,'' Clint said, nodding to the gun rack behind the man's desk. ''That'll make their intentions clear.''

''What are you gonna do?''

''Well, for one thing I'm gonna keep my girls off the street,'' Clint said. ''After that I'll wait and see what Swallow does. If things work out the way I want them to, I'll be able to sit down and talk to him.''

''And if they don't work out the way you hope?''

''I don't want to think about that right now, Sheriff,'' Clint said. ''We don't have the time.''

FORTY

"I'm not surprised," Jenny said.

"Why not?" Miriam asked. "I think it's horrible."

"I've been in towns before that didn't like whores," Kathy said. "This one takes the cake, though. He'd just leave us at Ben Swallow's mercy? Because to help us would risk his job? What kind of place is this?"

"The kind that closes down a whorehouse," Jenny said, "and puts the furnishings in the sheriff's office."

They were in Clint's room again, crowded into his bed. Looking at them, Clint thought, this is any man's dream, to have this many beautiful women on his bed. He wished that he had nothing better to do than to dive right into the midst of them.

"If you have to force him to help," Gloria asked, "how much help will he really be?"

"I don't know," Clint said. "Not much, I guess, but then maybe we don't need him to be."

"You really think you'll be able to talk some sense into Ben Swallow?"

"I may not have to."

"Why not?" she asked.

"Because," he said, "a man like Swallow responds to one thing."

"And what's that?" Rachel asked.

Clint looked at each of them in turn and then said, "Money."

There was a pause and then Jenny said, "Our money?"

"You mean you want to buy him off?" Gloria asked.

"It's the only way I can see to get you out of this," he said. "That is, unless you think Carthage will just send someone else after you."

"Well," Gloria said, "he's not going to take losing sixty-eight thousand dollars sitting down."

"Then send it back," Miriam said.

They all looked at her.

"That won't work, either," Gloria said. "His ego is hurt. He'll want more than just the money."

"Well, okay, then," Clint said. "We'll give him more than just money."

"You have an idea?" Gloria asked.

"Not really," he replied, "but with sixty-eight thousand dollars, maybe we can buy one."

"From who?"

"From somebody who knows him better than you do."

"Like who?"

"Like, maybe, Ben Swallow."

Clint instructed the women to remain inside the hotel, and then went out. From his vantage point he could see two men on either side of the street with rifles, and Sheriff Taylor in front of his office. Apparently, he'd had no trouble convincing his deputies to do their jobs, and no problem recruiting two more.

Clint crossed over and walked down to the office.

"I see you got four men," he said.

"You'd be surprised what mentioning your name will do," Taylor said. "They were all excited to be on the same side as you. They think we're gonna have another O.K. Corral."

"I hope you told them we'd like to get through this without a shot being fired."

"I told them."

"Did you tell them who we're up against?"

"They knew the name," Taylor said. "It made them even more excited to be siding with the Gunsmith against him."

"And you?"

"Me?" Taylor said. "I don't mind telling you I'm a little sick to my stomach. This is not Dodge City or Tombstone, you know. We don't usually have this kind of excitement."

"I admire you for admitting that, Sheriff," Clint said. "And I'm sorry I had to force you into this."

"Forget it," the lawman said. "You were right from the beginning; it is my job."

"I'm really going to try to get through this without any shooting."

"I hope you can do it," Taylor said.

Suddenly, they both heard the sound of horses, and then a group of men appeared at the end of the street. As they entered the street, they slowed their pace and walked their horses down the main drag. It was obvious that they saw the lawmen on either side.

Clint waited to see what they would do.

"Looks like they got the law on their side, Ben," Ab Nevers said.

"I can see that."

"What do we do?"

"They're only four of them," Zack Wilson said.

"Look again, half-wit," Ben Swallow said. "In front of the sheriff's office."

"So they're six," Wilson said. "We can still take 'em."

"Number one," Swallow said, "I ain't goin' up against the law, and number two, one of the men in front of the sheriff's office is Clint Adams."

Wilson squinted, then said, "Oh."

"Still want to take them on six against six?" Swallow asked him.

"It won't be fair," Wilson said, "not with the Gunsmith on their side."

"Then shut up from now on, Zack," Swallow said.

"Yessir."

"Ben?" Ab Nevers said.

"Let's stop in front of the saloon and go inside for a drink," Swallow said.

"And then what?" Nevers asked.

"And then the next move is Adams's."

Gloria and the girls had crowded around the window of Clint's room. They watched as Ben Swallow and his men walked their horses down the street.

"Jesus," Rachel said, "it's Ben."

"I see Caleb," Kathy said. "I know I could talk him out of this."

"You won't get the chance, Kathy," Gloria said. "Just remember, he works for Swallow."

"There's six of them," Jenny said. "Clint can't face six."

"He's got the sheriff and four deputies," Miriam said.

"They won't help him," Jenny said. "You watch."

"Then he'll be killed," Miriam said. "For us!"

"Stop worrying about him," Jenny said, "and start worrying about what will happen to us if they do kill Clint."

"What are they doing?" Ally asked. "I can't see."

"They're dismounting and going into the saloon," Gloria said.

"Why are they doing that?"

"I don't know," Gloria said. "I guess they don't want to have a shoot-out on the street."

"That's good, isn't it?" Ally asked. "Isn't that what Clint wanted?"

"That's what he said," Miriam chimed in, "but what will he do now?"

"I guess we'll just have to wait and see," Gloria said.

• • •

Clint and Taylor watched as Swallow and his men dismounted and went into the saloon.

"Why are they doin' that?" Taylor asked.

"Probably to get a drink," Clint said.

"Huh?"

"Also to get off the street."

"So what do we do now?"

"You do nothing," Clint said. "Make sure your men know that."

"And what are you going to do?"

"Well, it looks like I'm going to have the chance I wanted," Clint said.

"What's that?"

"To try and talk Ben Swallow out of this."

FORTY-ONE

When Clint walked into the saloon, Ben Swallow and his men had taken seats at three different tables. Swallow was sitting at one with one of his men. The other men had settled down at the other two. They all had beers in front of them, and they all had their eyes on Clint.

Clint walked over to where Swallow was sitting.

"Adams," the man said.

"Swallow."

"You got guts, walkin' in here like this," Swallow said. "It was a smart move, coming into this town and gettin' the law on your side."

"I got lucky," Clint said.

"They willin' to back you in a fight?"

Clint smiled.

"They think it's going to be another O.K. Corral," he said. "They're excited."

"They're fools, then," Swallow said. "Have a seat and we'll talk about this."

From Clint's vantage point he was able to see all of Swallow's men. If he took one of the two remaining chairs at the table, he wouldn't be.

"I'd rather stand."

"Suit yourself. Those women here with you? Or did you send them on?"

"They're here."

"Well, hand them over and there won't be any trouble, then."

"Afraid I can't do that."

"Why not?"

"They don't want to go back."

"Ted Carthage wants them back."

"You think Carthage sent you all this way to bring back six whores?"

"And a wagon," Ab Nevers said.

"Who's he?" Clint asked.

"Ab Nevers," Swallow said. "He's my second."

"Maybe he can get me a beer."

Nevers sat up straight and was about to answer, but Swallow put his hand on the younger man's arm.

"Get him a beer, Ab."

"But, Ben—"

"Do it!"

Nevers stood up, gave Clint a murderous look, and walked to the bar.

"Take his chair," Swallow said. "You can see the room from it."

Clint sat. Swallow was right. He could see everybody.

"Swallow—"

"Call me Ben," the other man said. "I'll call you Clint. Who knows? Maybe we'll end up friends."

"Do you know why Carthage wants those women and the wagon?"

"Well," Swallow said, "just between you and me, I think ego's got a lot to do with it."

"Ego," Clint said, "and sixty-eight thousand dollars."

That caught Swallow's attention. It also did not escape his attention that he was the only one who had heard what Clint said.

Ab Nevers returned then and put a beer down in front of Clint.

"You're in my seat."

"Go sit at one of the other tables, Ab."

"But, Ben—"

"Goddamn it!" Swallow said. "Do what I tell you for once, Ab!"

Fuming, Nevers walked away and sat down with Zack Wilson and Caleb Manson.

"He's your second, huh?"

"He's still young, but he's learnin'." Swallow leaned forward and lowered his voice. "Now, what's this talk about sixty-eight thousand dollars?"

"What's goin' on?" Wilson asked Nevers. "I can't hear what they're sayin'."

"Neither can I," Nevers said, "and I don't like it."

"What do you think is goin' on, Ab?" Manson asked.

"I don't like to think about it, Caleb," Nevers said. "It ever occur to you two that this is a lot of trouble to go to for six whores and a wagon?"

"Well, now that you mention it, yeah," Zack Wilson said.

"You sayin' somethin' else is involved?" Caleb Manson asked.

"I'm sayin' I think so."

"Like what?"

"The only thing I can of," Nevers said, "is money."

"You think these whores stole money from Carthage?" Wilson asked.

"He'd kill them for that!" Manson said.

"Yeah," Nevers said, "he would—if we brought them back."

"What are you sayin', Ab?" Manson asked.

Nevers looked away from the table where Clint and Swallow were talking and looked directly at the two men sitting with him.

"I'm sayin' if I make a move, will you be with me?" he asked.

"Against Adams?" Wilson asked.

"Or Ben?" Manson asked.

"Either," Nevers said, "or both."

"I don't know about goin' against Ben, Ab," Manson said.

"He's gonna dump you anyway, after this one," Nevers said.

"What? You mean—"

"He figured it out for himself, Caleb."

"Shit!"

"And me?"

"I had to tell him about what happened with the women in Gentry, Zack."

"So he's lettin' me go, too?"

"I'm afraid so."

"Fuck 'im, then," Wilson said. "You make a move, I'm your man, Ab."

"Caleb?"

"Me, too, I guess," Manson said. "What else is there to do?"

"Nothin'," Nevers said, looking back at Clint and Swallow, who were now chatting like bosom buddies, "nothin' at all."

FORTY-TWO

"You seen this money?" Swallow asked.

"No."

"You're takin' their word it's there?"

"Yes."

Swallow shook his head.

"I won't take nobody's word, Clint," Swallow said. "I got to see that money."

"I can arrange that," Clint said, "but we'd have to wait until dark. Can you get your men to agree to stay over-night?"

"Agree?" Swallow asked. "They don't agree, they just do what I tell them to do."

"Okay, then tell them you've decided to stay overnight. Get yourselves some rooms, and then meet me in the livery at midnight. I'll show you the money."

Swallow rubbed his jaw. He was getting way too old to be traipsing around the countryside and sleeping on the ground. His bones had been telling him that for months, but especially these past weeks. With sixty-eight thousand he could retire—especially if he didn't have to split it with anyone.

"You don't want any of the money?"

"No."

171

"What about Carthage?"

"What about him?" Clint said. "You tell me. What's he really want?"

"Well," Swallow said, "if I knew about the money, I'd say that was what he wanted. As it is I think he wants the whore, Gloria. She's the one who took the girls and the wagon, and now that I know about the money, I'm sure she took that, too. Yeah, he wants her."

"Well, here's the deal, then," Clint said. "You get the money, and you tell him she's dead."

"And what do I tell him about the wagon?" Swallow asked. "He wants that back."

"And if you take the money he's going to want to know where it went," Clint said. "Tell him a story."

"What kind of story?"

Clint shrugged.

"Tell him the wagon burned up somehow."

"With the money in it?"

"That's what he'll think," Clint said, "and he won't ask you about it, because you never knew."

Ben Swallow took a sip of his beer and set the mug down.

"This could work," he said.

"Sure, it could," Clint said, "and you and your men split sixty-eight thousand dollars."

"Oh, yeah," Swallow said, "split, sure. Listen, though, don't mention anything about the money to them. One of them might get greedy."

"Sure thing, Ben," Clint said. "It's just between you and me. What you do with your men is your business."

"Right," Swallow said, "my business."

Gloria and Ally were still at the window, with Rachel behind them. The other girls were sitting on Clint's bed, waiting impatiently.

"I hate to think about all that lovely money being given to Ben Swallow," Kathy said.

"How else are we all gonna stay alive, Kathy?" Miriam asked.

"I know," Kathy said. "I just wish there was another way."

"Well, there isn't," Gloria said. "This is the best way to go about this, and we're just going to have to face it. That money's gone."

"I wish I never even knew about it now," Ally said. "Be easier than losing it."

"Gloria?" Jenny said.

"Yeah?"

"Why *didn't* you tell us about the money?"

"I thought we went through that," Gloria said. "I didn't want any of you worrying about it. I was going to divide it up when we settled down someplace. Then we could have all done what we wanted to do."

"Uh-huh."

Gloria turned her head to look at Jenny.

"You don't believe me?"

"If you say so," she said, "it must be true. The rest of you believe it, don't you?"

"Well, sure," Ally said.

"Yeah," Kathy said.

"Definitely," Miriam said.

"See?" Jenny asked.

Gloria turned back to the window, not satisfied with the answer.

"They still in there?" Jenny asked.

"Still there."

"I keep thinkin' I'm gonna hear shots," Rachel said. "Lots of shots."

"Me, too," Ally said. "I'm cringing already."

"Clint will be all right," Miriam said, "he just has to be."

There was a moment of silence, and then Ally said, "As long as we don't hear shots."

"Let's hope we don't," Gloria said.

Inside, she was *praying* they wouldn't.

FORTY-THREE

"You're gonna *what*?" Gloria asked.

"Meet Swallow at midnight at the livery and show him the money."

"Why?"

"Because he won't deal until he sees it."

"And what kind of deal does he want to make?" Jenny asked.

"It's not what kind of deal *he* wants to make," Clint said, "it's what kind of deal *we* want to make."

"And that is?" Rachel asked.

"The money in return for telling Carthage that Gloria is dead."

"And what about the rest of us?" Jenny asked.

"When he realizes that Gloria is dead and the money is gone," Clint said, "he'll probably forget about the rest of you and let you go."

"But we can't be sure of that," Kathy said.

"We can't be sure of anything," Clint said, "but we've got to try something. If one of you has a better plan, let's hear it."

"Kill him," Jenny said.

"Kill who?" Clint asked. "Swallow? What would that accomplish?"

175

"Kill Carthage."

They all looked at her.

"It's what we should have done in the first place," she said.

"Oh, and which one of us was going to pull the trigger? You?"

"If we'd thought of it then, yeah," Jenny said, "I would have."

"So why didn't you think of it?" Ally asked.

"None of us thought of it," Gloria said, getting in the middle. "It wasn't an option."

"Then why don't we make it an option now?" Jenny asked.

"Are you gonna go back and kill him now?" Kathy asked.

"No," Jenny said, "we can hire Clint to do it."

"And use what to pay him?" Rachel asked.

"The sixty-eight thousand."

"It's too late for that," Clint said. "I've already told Swallow about the money. Besides, I don't hire my gun out. I don't kill people for money."

"Then we can hire somebody else," Jenny said.

"Didn't you hear what Clint said?" Kathy asked. "It's too late."

"Why? We haven't given the money away yet."

"As good as," Gloria said.

"Gloria," Jenny said, "after all this do you want to give that money up?"

"No," she said, "but we don't have a choice."

"Okay," Jenny said, "what if we offer Swallow half to kill Carthage?"

"I don't like paying somebody to kill somebody," Miriam said.

"Neither do I," Kathy said.

"So we just let Clint give the money away?"

"He's buying our freedom," Rachel said, "with money we didn't even know we had in the first place."

"Gloria knew," Jenny said.

"It's her money."

They all looked at Miriam, who had spoken.

"What?" Jenny asked.

"She stole it from him," Miriam said. "It's her money. She didn't ever have to tell us about it, but she was going to. I think it's up to her what happens to it."

They all continued to stare at Miriam for a few moments, and then Ally said, "I think Miriam's right. It is Gloria's."

"They're right," Kathy said, and they all agreed in turn until it came to Jenny.

"You're all crazy," she said and stormed out of the room.

"Somebody should go after her," Ally said.

"No," Gloria said, "leave her alone, for a while." She turned to Clint. "Give Swallow the money, if he'll agree to the deal."

"All right," Clint said. "I'll meet him at midnight and let you know what happens. Meanwhile, you girls better go back to your rooms."

They all left and Clint lay down on the bed, aware of the warmth they had all left behind.

FORTY-FOUR

Clint arrived at the livery at a quarter 'til midnight. He was aware that Swallow could have had all his men hidden in that barn, waiting for him to bring the money out, but in everything he'd ever heard about the man he'd never heard that he was a liar. Still, wasn't he prepared to cheat his men out of this money?

Duke was in the barn, though, and if there were other men around, the big gelding would not be standing so easily. Clint felt reasonably certain when he got there that he was alone.

He'd managed to get the key to unlock the barn by paying the liveryman some money. He'd also had the man bring the wagon inside. He lit a lamp that was hanging from a nail, then walked to the wagon, climbed inside, and followed Gloria's instructions to find the space where she'd hidden the money.

He pried up the floorboard she had told him about, reached in and felt around. For some reason he wasn't surprised when he found nothing. Had it ever been there? Or had someone recently removed it? Either way, he was now faced with the task of explaining to Ben Swallow that the money was gone.

"Adams," Swallow's voice called out in a loud whisper. "You here?"

"I'm here," Clint said and climbed down from the wagon. He came around it to face Swallow.

"Where's the money?" Swallow asked.

"About the money—"

"Sixty-eight thousand, you said," Swallow reminded him. "Ain't that what you said?"

Before Clint could answer a voice said, "Sixty-eight thousand? You were thinking of sharing that with us, weren't you, Ben?"

Clint and Swallow turned and saw three men entering the livery. One Clint recognized as Ab Nevers. Since he'd never met the other two, he didn't know that they were Caleb Manson and Zack Wilson. All three had their guns out.

"I can't believe it," Wilson said. "You was gonna cheat us out of our share, wasn't you, Ben?"

"Of course I wasn't," Swallow said. "Who told you that? Put those guns away."

"You ain't givin' the orders, Ben," Ab Nevers said. "I am."

"You takin' over, Ab?"

"That's right, Ben."

"How do the others feel about this?"

"The others don't have to know."

"So you're gonna cheat them?"

Nevers shrugged.

"Somebody's always cheatin' somebody, Ben."

"You said it," Clint replied.

"What's that mean?" Nevers asked.

"It's what I was about to tell Ben," Clint said. "Somebody cheated all of us."

"What are you talkin' about?" Nevers asked.

"The money's gone."

"What?" Swallow and Nevers said at the same time.

"Just what I said," Clint repeated. "It's gone."

"Sixty-eight thousand dollars?" Zack Wilson asked.

"Wait a minute," Nevers said. "How do we know you didn't come over here earlier and take it?"

"Yeah," Swallow said to Clint. "How do we know?"

"Because I'm telling you I didn't. How do we know Ben didn't come in here earlier and find it?"

"Yeah," Zack Wilson said. "How do we know that?"

"Look, boys," Swallow said, "it's Adams, not me. In fact, maybe there never was any money. Maybe he just got me here to kill me, and you boys just saved my life."

They all stood quietly for a moment, trying to work things out for themselves.

"What do we do, Ab?" Caleb finally asked.

"I'll tell you what we do," Swallow said before Nevers had a chance to respond. "We go back to the way things were. Adams lied about the money, probably to set us against each other. We got to pull together and do what we were being paid to do."

"And forget that you were gonna cheat us, Ben?" Nevers asked. "I don't think I can do that. How do we know you been tellin' us the truth all along about how much we been gettin' paid for jobs?"

"I ain't never cheated you boys!"

"Until tonight."

The way it was set up, Clint and Swallow were facing the other three, whose guns were already drawn.

"I guess they're figuring on killing us, Ben," Clint said.

"I guess so," Swallow said, "only I ain't so easy to kill."

Swallow went for his gun first, but it was Clint who was the first to clear leather. He shot Ab Nevers just as he shot Swallow. Before going down Ben Swallow shot Zack Wilson, and then Clint shot Caleb Manson just as Manson fired at Swallow and the older man was hit again. Just to be on the safe side Clint pulled the trigger three more times in rapid succession, putting one more bullet each into Nevers, Wilson, and Manson.

And then it was quiet.

Clint bent over Ben Swallow just in time to see the last glimmer of life go out in his eyes. He turned as he heard footsteps and then Sheriff Taylor entered with Gloria behind him.

"What the hell—" he said.

"Four dead men, Sheriff," Clint said.

"Are you all right?" Gloria asked Clint.

"I will be," Clint said, "as soon as we find out who took that money—that is, if there ever was any money."

"It's gone?"

"Was there, Gloria?" Clint asked. Quickly, with practiced efficiency, he ejected the spent shells, fed live ones into his gun, and holstered it. "Was there ever sixty-eight thousand dollars?"

"Sixty-eight . . . what?" Taylor asked.

"Oh, there was money, all right," Gloria said, "and if it's gone, I think I know who took it."

EPILOGUE

Clint and Gloria knocked on the door to the room Rachel was sharing with Jenny. Rachel was the one who opened the door, rubbing her eyes.

"What's goin' on?" she asked.

"Rachel, where's Jenny?"

"She's in here."

"We want to talk to her."

Rachel backed up so they could enter. There were two beds in the room, and Jenny was reclining on one, fully dressed. Rachel, however, was wearing a nightgown. She was making full use of the real bed while they had access to it.

"Now what? Another meeting?"

"Yes," Gloria said, "and we're having it right here."

"Where's the money, Jenny?"

"What?"

"Don't play dumb," he said. "You went storming out of the room earlier. You're the only one who could have gone to the livery stable and taken the money out of the wagon."

"Come on, Jenny," Gloria said. "Where is it?"

Jenny looked stubborn for a moment, then sat on the edge of the bed.

183

"I just didn't want you givin' it away."

"Well, you almost got Clint killed," Gloria said. "Didn't you hear all the shooting?"

"There's always shooting in a town."

"That was you?" Rachel asked.

"It was me," Clint said.

"Are you all right?" Rachel asked.

"He's lucky to be alive," Gloria said, "no thanks to you."

"Well, I'm sorry," Jenny said. "I didn't want anybody to get hurt."

"Well, four men are dead, Jenny," Clint said, "so where's the money?"

"It's under my bed."

"There's been sixty-eight thousand dollars under the bed all night?" Rachel asked.

"All evening, anyway," Jenny said. "Clint, I really didn't want you to get hurt."

"Never mind," Clint said. "Just let me have the money."

"What are you going to do with it?"

"Well, thanks to you we had a shoot-out in the livery stable and the sheriff came running. He knows all about the money."

"Is he gonna arrest us?" Rachel asked.

"No," Clint said. "He's agreed to send the money back to Carthage and tell him that Gloria was killed, also. That should keep him from looking for the rest of you."

Jenny bent over and pulled out the sack that Gloria had filled with the money.

"So we're gonna lose it, anyway," she said, pushing it over to him.

He picked it up and said, "At least Swallow's not going to get it."

"No," she said glumly, "Ted Carthage gets it back."

"Maybe he'll use it to hire some new whores," Gloria said. "At least we don't have to go back."

"So we can keep going to San Francisco?" Rachel asked.

"You can go anyplace you want," Clint said.

"Clint," Gloria said, "will you still take us there?"

"I said I would," he answered, "and I'll keep my word." He hefted the money and said, "I'd better keep this in my room until morning, and then I'll give it to the sheriff."

"How can you be sure he'll send it back to Carthage?" Jenny asked.

"I'll go to the bank with him before we leave and make sure," Clint said. "You girls better get some sleep."

Jenny pouted.

"You should be glad you didn't get us all arrested," Gloria said to her.

Clint and Gloria left the room and started down the hall toward theirs.

"Oh, damn," she said.

"What?"

"I don't have my key, and I don't want to wake Miriam up."

"No problem," he said. "You can sleep in my room."

"Really?"

"Sure."

"You don't mind?"

"No," he said as they reached his door. "I don't mind."

"But . . . your room only has one bed."

"Like I said," Clint repeated as they entered his room, "I don't mind . . . if you don't."

He closed the door and they turned to face each other.

"Oh, why not?" she asked. "I might as well win the bet tonight, too."

"What bet is that?"

"Well . . . I'm a little embarrassed about this, but we all had a bet about who would get to sleep with you first."

"Oh . . . I see."

"You're not mad?"

"No," he said, putting the bag of money down, "I'm not mad."

She came into his arms, and he wondered if she'd say the same thing when she found out she hadn't won the bet.

He wouldn't tell her, though, or any of the others. Not until they reached San Francisco. With a little luck, by then they'd all think they'd won.

Watch for

THE GAMBLER'S GIRL

205th novel in the exciting GUNSMITH series

from Jove

Coming in February!